View from the Hill: Monash Writers Anthology

By

Monash Writers Group

Tale Publishing

First Published 2016

National Library of Australia Cataloguing-in-Publication entry
Creator: Monash Writers Group, author.
Title:
View from the Hill: Monash Writers Anthology.
ISBN: 9780994439956 (paperback)
Subjects: short stories.
Dewey Number: 823.08

Cover image:
View of the Kiewa Valley from Mt Beauty
Watercolour by Gordon JR Smith

Tale Publishing
Melbourne Victoria

Contents

Introduction to the Anthology

Ask a member of Monash Writers Group why they write and you will hear a variety of emphatic responses:

'I want to be a published author.'

'I love playing with language; you know, picking it apart, then figuring out how to put it all back together again.'

'It's cathartic.'

'Writing allows me to be me.'

'I'm challenged by it – and that's a good thing!'

'Just for fun!'

At Monash Writers Group we've certainly had plenty of fun.

'So, I've got my story – but where should I begin?

'Challenge yourself – begin at the end!'

'Let's get to know your characters inside out, beyond what they do in your story. Let's place them into other situations and see how they respond then.'

‘Let’s hear stories from people who write in such different genres and see where we sit with that.’

As the facilitator of the group, I am often moved by what can emerge in a ten-minute writing session. How did that extraordinary piece of writing come within minutes, in a quiet, pen-quickened room? And oh my goodness, the poetry I have heard being read out in this room – Respect!

There’s a certain amount of bravery for even the most experienced writer to read their work out loud to twitching ears. We learn how to give critical feedback and understand that examining someone else’s work helps us evaluate our own writing. We are both giving and receiving.

Now, I hear you ask, what of this theme, this View from the Hill? Which hill?

Wheelers Hill, of course! Right where we meet, once a month, in the library, perched on Wheelers Hill. Once you find the right spot, the view rolls on for miles, until it is captured by the ranges beyond. You will discover as you read through the anthology that we applied this theme and then allowed that to be as broadly interpreted as the rolling view itself.

I have been wondering, what is the common noun for a group of eclectic writers? A quill of authors? A whirl of writers? A whorl, perhaps? Personally, I like a camaraderie of writers, of linguistic acrobats. Whatever the term may be, alongside our writing has emerged a bunch of people who respect each other’s craft, who give each other time, and who have fun together sharing what they love doing … writing!

Feel free to join us. Bring your pen and paper or

laptop if preferred, and most definitely your heart and soul.

Enjoy the fruits of our Monash Writers Group – each person's view from their own imagined hill.

Margaret Hepworth
Monash Writers Group Chairperson 2015-2016

The Voyeur on the Hill

Bishnu Addison

Maggie was at an age when she no longer attracted any attention or interest from people. She was content to sit on the balcony of her weatherboard home in Belgrave and use an old pair of binoculars to watch people in the suburbs below. 'I can't read anymore, even the large print is a challenge,' she complained, regretfully. 'But I enjoy watching the grey shadows of people and the traffic through these lenses. People's activity reassures me I'm still alive.' Although it was a harmless hobby it made her feel like a voyeur. Still, she continued to indulge in her hobby, which she preferred to call "People Spotting".

One sunny afternoon the blinding reflection from the window of a little cottage in Tecoma caught her attention. 'Have to wait for Sally to provide me with information,' she muttered, but the wait wasn't very long. Sally called out from the front door, ‘Hello Maggie. Are we going shopping or have the ladies from the church stocked up your pantry and fridge on Saturday?’ Instead of answering, Maggie pointed her bony finger towards the little cottage and asked, ‘Sally, who lives in that dear little cottage?’ Sally followed the direction of the pointing finger. ‘Which cottage, the one with a picket fence and a birdbath in front?’

Maggie replied good humouredly, ‘I don’t know dear. If I could see that clearly with my dodgy eyes, I wouldn’t ask would I?’ Sally realised her error, and in an effort to make amends, inquired in a softer tone, ‘Why do you want to know?’

‘Only idle curiosity, dear!’

Recognising a perfect opportunity to share a bit of local gossip and stall doing the chores, Sally promptly said, ‘Maggie how about I make us a pot of tea? I brought some blueberry muffins from Bakers’ Delight. We could have them with your English Breakfast tea while I tell you all about the occupants of your favourite cottage.’

‘Run along then, and put the kettle on.’ Maggie heard the clatter of crockery in the kitchen and was afraid more fine china might be chipped. She raised her feeble voice and cried out, ‘Do be careful with the crockery dear, they are my dear late mother’s wedding present. I’d hate to see them all chipped and cracked.’ Sally ignored the warning and continued preparing the morning tea. Once everything was laid on the tray, she took it out to the balcony where Maggie sat. The old lady looked up and was delighted to see the tray laden with treats. Her pale face broke into a childlike smile, adding more wrinkles on her face and exposing her gum with two missing front teeth.

Buttering the warm muffins, Sally resumed, 'What do you want to know about the people in the yellow cottage?'

'Just wanted to know who lived there. I see a dark cloud hanging over the cottage. I don't see many visitors either. My intuition tells me they are experiencing some grave sadness.'

'Our resident psychic has heard voices in her head again, has she?' teased Sally, who knew Maggie liked to test her supernatural power and was elated if her prediction was correct or even remotely close to the truth. They both focused their attention on the cottage as they enjoyed their morning tea.

Sally drank her hot cup of tea, brushed the muffin crumbs off her jumper and proceeded to unravel the sad tale of George and Hanna Brown. 'They were married in a quaint little local church surrounded just by family and close friends. Hanna had made a lovely bouquet for herself at the florist where she worked. George received a handsome bonus from the accounting firm where he was a book keeper. They didn't go on a honeymoon. Hanna suggested to George that they should save that money to build a nursery for the baby they planned to have in the not so distant future. Life was blissful; George was pleased with his new bride. She had all the attributes of a loving wife, plus was a supportive partner who would undoubtedly make an excellent mother for his children. She was a very practical woman and was aware of her body clock ticking away, so the plan to start their family was paramount in her mind. She loved George dearly and wanted to have his children and raise them in the little cottage, away from the city madness of heavy traffic and pollution. Both were only children and had suffered from loneliness, so her plan was to have two children regardless of their gender.'

But alas! The brilliant wedding day had gradually faded into oblivion and each of them drowned themselves in their work. The longing for a child became stronger and more urgent with the passing of time. Wedding anniversaries were tactfully ignored or deliberately forgotten. There was no sign of Hanna falling pregnant. Although, they were still in love, the unfulfilled desire of parenthood began to fester like an incurable wound. The need for a child became an unhealthy obsession threatening their marriage. Every evening George would arrive home and call out from the door, 'Hello love, I'm home. How's your day?' The reply was always the same, 'Nothing exciting to tell, George. It was fairly quiet. Perhaps the wedding season is over. Business is slow.'

The zest had disappeared from her life. The bubbly woman he had married no longer existed; the new Hanna was always tired and preoccupied. After work he would sit in front of the TV nursing a can of beer while she prepared their meal in silence. On a clear day Maggie would see the ageing Holden parked in the driveway and knew George was home. Hanna chose to ride her bike to work claiming, 'Bike riding keeps me fit and healthy'. But family and friends knew she was saving money to build a nursery for the dream child, or

IVF treatment which was way beyond their financial reach. However, she had not abandoned hope of bearing a child.

Over the years Hanna saw several gynaecologists who made the same diagnoses. 'You are perfectly healthy, Mrs Brown. Be patient. Some woman take longer to conceive.' All she could do was thank them politely and return home disappointed. In order to avoid a barrage of intrusive questions such as, 'When are you starting a family?' Followed by, 'Don't leave it too late. Bringing up little children requires plenty of energy,' they chose whenever possible to avoid socialising. Unfortunately, at one dinner party which they could not get out of, a tactless guest remarked, 'Perhaps you should both have a thorough medical checkup followed by proper treatment urgently. It is obvious neither of you are getting any younger.' The thoughtless remark hurt her deeply. She wanted to storm out, but societal etiquette restrained her. She heaved a sigh of relief when the party was over and they could all depart.

Hanna got into their car and sat quietly dabbing her eyes and runny nose with tissues. The seed of doubt was planted in their mind by the self-righteous guest. George began to suspect that Hanna might be infertile and Hanna on the other hand began to think George might be sterile and the cause of her failure to become pregnant. This was a dangerous situation to be in. The love and trust they shared was being threatened, and the blame game was so easy to play. Each longed for a child and began to suspect the other to be at fault. They drove home in silence, wallowing in their own misery and suspicion. Finally, they entered their picket fence gate. George cleared his throat and said in an assumed light heartedness, 'Home again.' He got no response. Obviously still very upset, Hanna ran into the house and straight into their bedroom while George watched her disappear down the hallway.

Maggie was surprised at the in-depth information Sally had gathered about the Browns. Unable to contain her amazement, she asked, 'How do you know so much about their private life, dear?'

Sally replied in a nonchalant manner, 'Those days I used to clean for Mrs. Higgins who lived next door to the Browns. She was a mine of information; she knew everything about the folks in Tecoma and the surrounding suburbs. She shared the information with me during our weekly chat over a cup of tea.'

Having heard more than she had bargained for, Maggie pointed out. 'It's time you did some housework, dear. Run along now, it'll be lunch time soon.'

Sally had no desire to resume her daily chores, so she put a tantalizing question to Maggie. 'Don't you want to know how it all ended?'

'Oh all right, make it brief,' ordered Maggie impatiently.

Having won her case, Sally continued to unravel the sad human misfortune with even greater enthusiasm. Finally, when she stopped to take a breath Maggie told her in a rather firm tone 'I have heard enough dear.

Now get some work done. It'll be your home time soon.'

Sally had run out of excuses to linger on and reluctantly resumed her duties. Maggie on the other hand continued to sit and reflect on the sad tale of Hanna and George.

Her intuition told her that unless Hanna miraculously fell pregnant soon this marriage would undoubtedly fail; it was only a matter of time. Dwelling on this sad possibility Maggie recalled her own past.

A voice in her head claimed, 'Once, I too was young and attractive. I worked for the typing pool in a local factory. One Valentine's Day I received a card from a secret admirer, but the office gossip found out it was Jack, so she told everyone. He was young and vulnerable. I never saw him again. He never came anywhere near me. On a rare trip to Phillip Island with some friends, she had met a young soldier on leave from Puckapunyal Army Training Camp. They had exchanged addresses and begun to correspond. One day she was held up at work. Before she arrived home, Mother had gone to the letter box and found a letter addressed to Maggie. As soon as she entered the front door she yelled, 'Who is this letter from, Maggie? You don't know anyone outside Belgrave!'

'Just a friend, Mother.'

'A young man I suppose. What's his job?'

'He's a soldier.'

'Why would you befriend a soldier? He'll probably go to war and get himself killed leaving you with half a dozen children. Get rid of him at once, do you hear me?' bellowed her mother. That was the end of her budding romance. She was an elderly spinster now who often amused herself by stepping into the "What if?" land.

She felt like Alice going down the rabbit hole in 'Alice in Wonderland' What if she had defied her mother and continued her friendship with her soldier? Would he have proposed? Would they be happily married with six children?' It was only an unfulfilled dream never to materialise in this lifetime. Gradually, her friends had got married and moved to fancier suburbs, leaving her with her ageing parents in Belgrave.

Eventually she had to give up work to look after them. Father had a stroke and the early stages of dementia. Maggie and Mother had to look after him twenty four hours a day. He suffered for ten long years. At the end he had a massive heart attack and died in his wife's arms. Although his death brought sadness, Maggie had some respite. Unfortunately, it lasted only a few months, because her mother fell down the stairs and broke her hip. However, she refused to spend time at the rehab and she insisted she would be better off at home, looked after by Maggie. 'Her father and I did enough for her. It's her turn to show some gratitude and look after me,' pointed Mother, to the authorities and came home. Maggie lovingly took care of her but Mother gradually turned into a cantankerous shrew demanding constant attention and food. One day, Dr. Hogan came to check on her and said, 'Maggie you are feeding your mother too well. She has put on a lot of weight. It's bad for her general health. She is not sick, get her out of bed and make her do some exercise round the house. Here's her prescription for blood pressure. She doesn't need any other medication. She is stronger than you. Just cut down on her snacks.' On that note he picked up his surgical bag and left.

Hearing the front door close, Mother rang the bell, demanding, 'Where's my morning tea? I'm parched,' she complained. Maggie ground her teeth and clenched her fists in frustration and went to the kitchen to prepare a pot of tea which she carried into her Mother's bedroom. Mother took one look at the tray and yelled. 'Are you planning to starve me to death? Didn't you bake any cake or scones?'

Unable to keep silent, Maggie repeated what Dr. Hogan had told her about the danger of indulging in too many snacks.

'How dare the quack encourage you to disobey me. This is my house and you'll do as I tell you or go find yourself another accommodation.'

The suggestion was deeply wounding. Maggie realised the only way to placate mother was to give her a generous supply of cakes and slices even though she knew they were bad for her health. She silently placed the loaded morning tea tray beside her bed, and left muttering under her breath, 'One day I will smother her with a pillow and claim she died of a heart attack in her sleep. Shocked at this wicked thought, she crossed herself and whispered, 'Holy Mother of God where did that criminal idea come from?' She had no answer. She was shaking like a leaf, so had to sit down to calm herself before clearing the morning tea tray. When she entered the bedroom, there was Mother sleeping like a baby. Maggie was full of remorse, 'How could I harm a fragile helpless, old lady, my own mother?' she remarked. and shamefully admitted, 'I'm turning into a bitter, intolerant woman. In future, I must never dwell on those unholy thoughts.'

The cool breeze woke her from reverie. She noticed her lunch was waiting on a tray, Smoke was swirling from the bowl of pumpkin soup and the freshly baked meat pie was begging to be eaten. Sally's heavy footstep was heard trampling around trying to vacuum the thread bare carpet. Obviously she was trying to finish all the chores before going home. Once Maggie confided in her social worker, 'Like all young people Sally likes to do as little as possible. On the other hand, when she puts her mind to it she is not a bad worker. Despite being an incurable gossip she's extremely honest and kind. I couldn't do without her.'

Winter gave way to spring. The little garden was awash with bloom. There was an invasion of bees, butterflies and cicadas. The sun was getting warmer. This encouraged Maggie to sit on her balcony well after sunset and observe the activities around the cottage. Many months had passed under her watchful eyes, but apart from the pretty flowers bursting open in their full glory attracting the birds and bees there was no sign heralding any change around the cottage. An uncanny chill ran down her curved spine, 'Good Lord,' she uttered. 'Don't tell me they have already broken up!'

She tried to focus her tired old eyes through her binoculars, in an effort to see through their curtain, only to admit in frustration, 'It's no good. I can't see through the curtain. All my senses are abandoning me.' Despite being utterly dejected by her mounting disabilities, she continued to gaze towards the cottage to bring herself back to reality.

Suddenly the lights in the Brown's home came on. Maggie focused harder, and saw two dark figures embracing, 'That's better,' she exclaimed in great joy. She concentrated harder. To her horror they were not embracing as she previously thought; they were having a punch up. Then one of them broke free and ran to the next room, rummaged through a drawer and pulled out an object, pointed to the temple and fired. Bang! It was a deafening shot. Maggie let out a blood curdling scream, "Oh noooo." She called out, 'Sally, come quick. No call the police! Never mind the police, call an ambulance! Something dreadful has happened.'

Sally responded with slight irritation in her voice, 'What's the matter? Did you spill hot tea all over you, or did you see an accident on Belgrave–Ferny Creek Road?'

Maggie rebuked her sharply, 'Nothing, as simple as that, you silly girl! It's the Browns. One of them has committed suicide. I heard the gun go off.'

'You heard a car backfire, Maggie. You were dozing off when I brought your afternoon tea.' Then added in a rather superior tone, 'Why would either one commit suicide when the long awaited dream baby is due within months.'

Maggie was shocked and jubilant at the same time.

She queried Sally's announcement

'What makes you so sure?'

'Last week Mrs. Higgins told me. Apparently both are ecstatic, and have resumed building and furnishing the nursery.'

'A child in spring. How wonderful. They can name her after one of the flowers in bloom.'

It was Sally's turn to challenge, 'How do you know it's going to be a girl?'

Maggie responded in her most regal voice, 'My psychic powers never fail me.' She continued as though in a trance, 'Abandoned by youth but embraced by old age and decrepitude, I still marvel at our ability to procreate and save the human race from extinction. It was a long and painful wait but they have accomplished their mission. I offer my gratitude to the Browns and rejoice with them.'

Table of Fate

Nikki Bielinski

Bree was first in line at the fortune teller's tent. She stared at the runic symbols of old magic on the protective entrance drapes, wanting to be called in. She shivered in the frosty night air, chilled to her heart.

It was the Winter Fair on Pendle Hill, a night when anything could happen. She had to find out the truth, especially as this night had cost her so dearly. She rubbed her hands together, trying to warm up.

'It's cold out here, isn't it?' said a voice behind her.

Bree turned around. 'Yes, it's freezing.'

A young couple smiled back at her. Suddenly self-conscious, Bree pulled the shawl over her head, staying in the shadows. She missed having long hair to conceal her face.

The girl shivered, her teeth chattering.

'Here, have my jacket,' said the boyfriend. He draped his tweed coat over his petite girlfriend. She snuggled him affectionately.

‘Enter,’ the fortune teller called.

“I wish we were next,” said the girlfriend.

‘I won’t be long,’ said Bree.

‘Take your time. We have the view from the hill. The lights in the Valley of Pendle are beautiful tonight. Besides, I’ll keep you warm,’ said the man. He gave a toothy, dental-whitened grin.

His girlfriend giggled and grabbed his arm. She looked up at him, her eyes shiny with happiness, reminding Bree of the love she’d lost.

She turned away from their loved-up bliss, their intoxication on ‘Cupid's charm’. Feeling very alone, she tentatively pushed aside the blood-red drapes and stepped in.

The drapes fell shut, muffling the voices and merry-go-round music of the fair. She was in, safe. The deal she’d cast had worked. There would be consequences, but she would face them later, if she had to.

A haze of incense cloaked her like a shroud. A lone pillar candle, like the ones they had in her hometown church, burned steadily. Bree winced and turned her back on the holy flame.

Silver stars and crescent moons hung from the canopy. She walked across a Turkish carpet towards the beautiful, dark eyed fortune teller. Bree’s chest tightened with pain.

‘Please, sit down.’

She sank into the protection of the armchair. She kept her shawl over her face, blocking out the flame of the candle.

‘So you tell people about their lives?’

‘Yes. I’m a fortune teller. What it says on the tent.’

Brusque and to the point. This beautiful, raven-haired woman, still of child bearing age didn’t seem to care. She had a cross-my-palm-with-silver kind of attitude.

'Payment first.' She stretched out her hand. Long elegant fingers, soft, warm flesh.

She didn't say please, but Bree gave her a cold, folded bank note anyway.

The fortune teller smiled and briskly stowed it in the deep in the folds of her silk robe.

'Call me Madame Elle. I can tell your future—today, tomorrow and forevermore. This is the table of fate.' She had the voice of a bluesy jazz singer who'd spent many late nights in bars.

Bree shivered uncontrollably. She tucked her icy hands under a fold in the velvet tablecloth. She looked into the dark eyes of Madame Elle.

She swallowed. For the first time she wondered if this was a good idea, then banished the thoughts to the back of her mind. Now was not the time for doubts.

Tarot cards, a fist sized crystal ball, and a crooked birch wand, were lined up on the red velvet tablecloth.

Across the table of fate she saw the fortune teller's beauty lit by the lamp's silvery sheen.

A cold draught whispered through the heavy, protective drapes. The candle-flame flickered. Bree flinched, as though scorched.

'Love life, is it?'

Bree bit her lip.

'Ahh, I see. Don't want to tell? That's fine. The cards know everything about love.' She reached for the Tarot cards with her ruby ringed hand.

'Love is dead,' said Bree. Her voice dry, wispy.

'Love lives where the heart beats. But we all see the future as painted by our past.' She narrowed her eyes, scrutinizing Bree. 'Perhaps you'd prefer the crystal ball?'

Bree shook her head.

‘What then?’

Irritation was in her voice. Bree knew of this woman’s reputation for anger.

She held out her hands.

‘Ahh. Palm reading. I can see a lot on palms. You may not be able to handle it. You need to be strong for this.’

Bree's left eye twitched. She put her hand over it, trying to stop the unrelenting flicker. ‘I need you to tell me the truth.’

‘I have many mystic powers. If the information I give you is too much, you must ask me to stop.’

Bree nodded.

Elle ran her hands over the red velvet tablecloth, rings glittering in the light.

‘I invite you to place your palms on the table of fate. Are you left or right handed?’

‘Left.’

‘So, your right hand is your fate and your left is what you choose to make of your life. Your index finger, is the finger of what you want in life, your destiny…’

‘I've heard this before. Get to the point, quickly please.’

There was a fire spark of anger in Madame Elle’s eyes. Then she looked down and traced the lines on Bree’s right palm.

‘I see a lot of music in your life. Your boyfriend, your ex-boyfriend, is a jazz musician. You have a very strong headline in your left hand, and no lifeline after the age of thirty. You're more than that now, aren't you?’

Bree shrugged. ‘You're the fortune teller. You tell me.’

Elle took a sharp breath in, as if to retort back. But

she thought better of it, smoothed down the black silk of her dress and glared at Bree.

'Despite having murderous attempts on your life, you pulled yourself together and decided to live. Your mind is more powerful than your mapped out destiny.'

Bree laughed.

'Are you here for my advice, or to mock me?'

Elle glanced over her shoulder, and then at Bree. She kissed her index finger and touched the heavy gold cross hanging around her neck.

'Show me your left hand.'

Jaw clenched tight, Bree held out her left hand, in a fist.

Elle grabbed Bree's fist and prised her fingers open. She held her palm under the lamp.

'You have no lifeline. You should not be alive,' whispered Elle.

'I have been wandering the world, trapped in a limbo since I was murdered,' hissed Bree.

'You shouldn't be here! You are a ghost enlivening your own corpse! How did you get through the protective drape magic?' She scraped back her chair and shoved against the table, trying to run, but Bree grabbed her. She yelped in surprise as Bree's cold fingers burned into her wrist, then stopped struggling, as though realising the futility of fighting.

'Yes, I needed to re-enliven my body, to do what I need to do.'

'The last ghost I saw who made it through the protective magic in an enlivened corpse, had done a deal … with HIM.'

Bree cackled. 'So I have done a deal with HIM. I have tonight, only tonight.'

Elle whimpered in fear.

'Don't be scared,' said Bree softly, reassuringly, 'I

have come to you to find out the truth. If you tell me the truth, you can't be in danger, can you?'

Elle gulped, shook her raven black hair and straightened up. 'I have told no lies, so I have no need to fear the truth.'

'Good.' Bree smiled at her across the table of fate.

Still looking her in the eyes and smiling, Bree's ghost lurched out of her body and lunged into Elle's.

Memories and destinies hit Bree like trucks on a highway. Sharp pangs of pain and electric flashes of joy shot through her mind. A wedding, a baby, being in front of the fireplace with her lover, it was all there. Bree gasped and struggled as she worked herself through the mind of another. She dragged her ghost form through the heat of the pumping arteries and blood rich organs of the woman. Bree saw the seed of cancer that would one day grow in the woman's breast in ten years, if … if she could survive tonight.

And there tucked away in the recess of slamming doors and locked cupboards of her mind, Bree saw the proof.

The fire. The same fire that had been in her home, in her house.

Shrieking with rage, Bree dragged herself out of the bodily heat and into the bitter, frosty cold of her own slumped body. She wondered how anyone as evil as Elle could have the warmth of humanity?

Bree shrugged into her skin once more, wriggling fingers and toes as though into gloves and socks. But they were appendages of no warmth.

She lifted her head and stretched her arms, heavy and awkward. Bree stared across the table at Elle, pale and jerking in pain as she recovered from having being possessed. Panting, she lifted her eyes to look into Bree's.

'You did it,' Bree croaked.

'Did what?' Elle gasped. She grabbed the table, trying to support herself.

'Burned me alive.'

'Bree Wilson?'

'What did you expect? You killed me to be with my Paul.' Bree pulled off her shawl, revealing her ghostly grey, burned and melted skin.

'It wasn't me. He did it. He gave you the sleeping pills in the cocktails.'

'Who lit the flame of the candle and kicked it over?'

Silence.

Bree pointed her index finger, the finger of destiny at Elle.

'TRUTH. NOW.'

She recoiled in horror, grabbed the gold cross that hung around her neck and thrust it up.

'A gold cross won't work on me! That isn't scary stuff,' Bree hissed.

'You tried to poison him when he said he wanted to leave you! It was an accident when the candles were knocked over and the house burned down.'

'That was no accident! You burned me alive and forced me into this hellish limbo. Now I want revenge!'

'There are other ways of finding revenge,' sobbed Elle.

'I'm not interested in another way. I'm only interested in this way.'

Bree sprang up and plunged her ghost hand deep into the woman's chest cavity. She squeezed her icy fingers around the woman's life source and crushed her pumping heart.

Elle's face contorted in pain. Bree gritted her rattling teeth and squeezed the fluttering heart more tightly. Elle's red lips turned dusky blue, then purple and finally grey.

She dropped, lifeless to the old Turkish carpet.

Bree crouched by the dead woman's body and kept a deathly grip on her flaccid heart. Sobbing, she stayed there until Elle's spirit rose up. Like a breath of glittering air, the woman's form rose and shivered through the night.

There was a faint scent of magnolia in the air.

'She will rest in peace, dammit,' groaned Bree.

She glared at the corpse. Then released her grip of the lifeless heart and withdrew her hand from the cold, thickening hold of rigor mortis.

Grabbing the birch wand from the floor, she pointed it sky high.

'Take me to the place of my ultimate revenge, like you promised I could!'

The wand tip combusted into flame and she burned a path like a rocket through the tent.

'Paul, it's your turn now. Be prepared to meet my wrath!' cried Bree. Like a shard of electric blue she shot through the night sky, scattering sparks of fire.

Bree's corpse was left behind, slumped across the carpet. A horned beast crawled out of the crystal ball and sprang on the unhappy remains.

Waiting outside the tent, the young couple clutched at each other, staring at the shower of fiery sparks scattering across the night sky.

'What's that streak of flaming sparks, sweetheart?' asked the girlfriend.

'Darling, that is…' the toothy, doting man struggled to make something up, '… that is Cupid, going to fulfil love's quest.'

Journey of Perception

Sasha Buntman

This morning, Hilda chose to dress completely in orange. 'Well, it is almost Halloween. And it feels like a bright orange day to me. What do you think, JoJo?' she murmured to Josephine, her elderly cat.

Josephine glared back at her with disinterest as she watched Hilda adjust her multi-coloured, vintage glasses on her wrinkly little nose. 'Ah, don't look at me like that! You know me. Life's too short to be boring. And that means having fun with what I wear!'

Sliding into a stylish, floral, orange frock, Hilda said, 'Remember this little number, JoJo? I found it at that classy op shop across the road from Pearl's flat.' She squeezed into the dark orange shoes that used to be her mother's. 'Which reminds me, JoJo. I will have to give that boring, predictable sister of mine a call today, to remind her to feed and care for you while I'm away.'

Accessories were the easy part: a fluffy pillbox hat, lots of beaded costume jewellery, a cameo brooch, and an antique, embroidered handbag. Most importantly, she applied a deep orange-red lipstick with smoky eye shadow. 'Okay, I'm ready to face the world. Have a delightful day, JoJo. I'll be back this afternoon, to finish packing.' Hilda was finalising the details of her big round the world trip. This required an outing to the city, to see her travel agent.

Hilda strolled through the hilly suburban streets to the local train station. The view from a hill was breathtaking, with the sun shimmering through the emerald trees. Savouring the beauty, Hilda smiled at a few strangers on her way.

When she arrived at the train station, she noticed there would be a fifteen-minute wait until the next train, so she dialled her sister's number on her obsolete Motorola phone. Pearl was Hilda's only living relative.

'Pearly, dear. How are you on this splendid day? Yes, I leave tomorrow morning. So excited to go on this magnificent adventure around the world, as a vagabond! I'm finally living the dream, dear. I've never been happier. I just wanted to remind you once again, to look after JoJo for me. I really do appreciate it, Pearly.'

Many years ago, Hilda reluctantly tolerated her sister, the 'favourite' daughter in the family. Pearl was constantly praised and adored. But quite some time ago, Hilda decided it was time to move on from the past, and stop holding grudges.

Pearl sounded genuinely concerned, her throat raspy and nasally. 'Hilly, of course, I won't forget about JoJo. It's not a problem. But I am still worried about you travelling alone. I know you say how happy you are, but sometimes it seems like you're just running away from reality.'

'It may seem that way, dear. But I've never had

children or a marriage to worry about. I have the freedom to do as I please, and that is what I intend to do. It's what I've always done. You know I'm not like you used to be. Remember how you used to always do everything you were told, that Mum and Dad wanted you to do – everything expected?' said Hilda, while admiring her rainbow-coloured nail-varnish and matching beaded bracelet. She relished being the black sheep of the family. 'Yes, I've always done whatever makes me happy, not what Mum or Dad or society persuaded me to do. I've followed my heart and soul. Perhaps I did what was considered dangerous, unconventional and wrong.' Hilda never needed anyone to make herself happy, as long as she had herself. Luckily, she has always enjoyed her own company.

'Yes, you know that I've always envied you, Hilly. Chasing your dreams, living by your own rules. But how long will you be away? I don't think you will be able to afford to stay away for long. What will you do when your money runs out? Fashionistas and artists don't make much money,' fretted Pearl.

'Oh, don't worry your pretty little head about such things, Pearly. I'll be just fine. I may be a 'little old lady' but I'm not stupid. I have saved up a sufficient amount. I'd say I'll be away for at least three months, all going well.'

Sitting elegantly on the train, with an aura of contentment, Hilda relished this time to seriously relax. From her Mary-Poppins-style handbag, she fished out her knitting needles, yarn, a Hello Kitty notebook and her round-the-world travel guide. Hilda occupied herself gleefully, inserting her earphones and listening to Enya on her mini-radio.

Finally arriving in the city, Hilda strolled towards her travel agency. It was in a large building, on the 12th floor.

'Good morning.' The travel agent's receptionist greeted Hilda with a bright and bubbly tone.

Hilda smiled. 'Morning. I have an appointment with Sally at 10.30 am.'

'Please take a seat. Sally will be with you shortly.'

Hilda sat on the foyer couch.

'You're getting excited, no doubt, Hilda?' said Sally as she approached. An experienced travel agent, Sally was just as passionate about the world as Hilda was. 'Here are all your documents. Your itinerary, tickets and other details. Remember, I'm always a text, phone call or email away if you get into any strife.'

'Thanks, Sally dear, you're a real gem. Oh, I'm extremely thrilled about all the different countries I'm going to explore. I just can't believe it, after all these years, I'm finally fulfilling my dream of travelling around the world. I'm going to feel like a glorious gypsy, aren't I?' Hilda was daydreaming as she spoke, with wonder in her eyes.

'Oh, yes,' smiled Sally. 'Very gypsy-like indeed. And I'm loving today's outfit.'

'Thanks, my dear. You do know my sister's a bit concerned about how I will cope on my own. I've given her your details. I told her she can contact you in case of any issues. You know I can take care of myself. She's just a worry wart. Everything's going to be divine, dear.'

'No worries at all. Pearl can talk to me anytime. Best of luck, Hilda. I look forward to seeing you on your return. Don't forget to share your photos and journal entries.' Sally walked Hilda out of her office, waving goodbye.

Hilda glanced around as she waited for the next elevator. A grungy looking teenage girl with raven black hair was also waiting.

Once inside the elevator, they each pressed the relevant buttons.

Suddenly the elevator made a huge thud—a loud, clanking noise. The sound was intense and startling.

'Looks like the lift is stuck,' said Hilda. 'We're in mid-air at the moment.'

The girl seemed shocked and puzzled. 'Let's try the emergency button.'

Hilda pressed it a few times but nothing happened. 'It's not working. It must be broken. Normally the button would light up. There's a phone number here. Do you have enough battery in your phone to make a call? Looks like my phone's dead,' she said, looking down at her old Motorola. After calling Pearl, it didn't have much juice left.

The girl dialled the emergency number right away. 'It's ringing … but no one is answering at the moment. I'll keep trying.'

'Oh dear. Well, since we're here and waiting until we're found we might as well introduce ourselves, hey? said Hilda. 'I'll start. I'm Hilly, a fashion-obsessed artist. My work focuses on living sustainably and frugally. I collect vintage clothes and accessories. My other passion is travel!'

The girl smiled. 'How fascinating. I'm Autumn Rain. I work at the antique shop over on Elizabeth. Old things … are also my passion.' She stared at Hilda's vintage outfit.

'What a lovely name you have,' Hilda observed, wondering if it was her real name or a nickname. 'So pretty! Of course I adore the season too. Autumn really is breathtaking.'

'I'm also a university student,' Autumn mumbled quietly.

'And … what are you studying, my dear?'

'Well, it's a bit complicated. At first, it was a science degree, and then I did a few arts subjects and found I quite enjoyed those too. So I've settled for Computer Science with a minor in Philosophy. I think,' Autumn nervously explained, while pushing her purple glasses into place.

Autumn started acting rather odd, staring at the ground. Her face was not visible at all, just a massive blob of untidy black hair. She clutched her bag tightly. Her eyes sparkled with the first hint of a tear that she was attempting to hold back.

Hilda was daydreaming again, but quickly returned her focus to Autumn. 'Is everything okay, dear?'

'In all honesty, no. I actually suffer from claustrophobia. If we stay in here for too much longer, it'll flare up! I'm already feeling really scared. Terrified in fact.' Autumn's face turned crimson, while sweat saturated her forehead. 'I'm suffocating. I need air! I've seriously got to get out of here, now!'

'Oh, dear. You poor thing! Here, have some cold water.' Hilda handed Autumn a water bottle. 'How long have you had claustrophobia?' Hilda inquired.

'It's been worse since my sister passed away, but I've always had a bit of it my whole life. As children, our parents left us alone in the car quite regularly. That's apparently when the phobia developed. I was seeing a specialist about it in the building today, actually.'

Without warning, Autumn fainted, flopping down on the metallic floor. Gently, Hilda sprinkled her forehead with water and she became mindful again.

'What can I do to help? How can claustrophobia be

treated?' asked Hilda.

'It's a challenging journey. My doctor's looking into cognitive therapy, to change my thoughts and reduce my anxiety levels. We may also try hypnotherapy, counter conditioning and breathing exercises. I refuse to use any medications. Only natural treatments,' Autumn said weakly.

'I'm not sure if you'll believe me, but I promise you that elevators are not dangerous. They're very useful in getting people from A to Z faster,' Hilda said, attempting to relieve Autumn's anxiety.

'You see, my older sister died a year ago. She was also my best friend and the only family member I had left,' Autumn said, a single tear running down her face.

'Oh, dear, I'm very sorry to hear that.' Hilda attempted to comfort Autumn by putting her arm around her.

'You know, I'm not a doctor but art and fashion have been a huge coping mechanism for me. When I lost a close friend just the other month, I threw myself into my art to focus my sad energies into something where I could express myself.' Hilda daydreamed about her deceased friend. She visualised Merle's spirit in the elevator with them as she spoke.

'Well, I have been writing poems lately … especially haikus. I suppose poetry's considered an art form, isn't it? It seems to get my mind off my sister and my phobias.' Autumn opened her backpack and handed a notebook to Hilda. She read a few lines to herself:

Painful loneliness
Anxious
Courage to face my fears and tears.

A lack of control

Empty
Feelings of pursuing dreams.

Illness and feeling
Nervous
I cannot cope any more.

I clear my mind by
Writing
Poems: to analyse thoughts.

'Wow, they're very evocative of your moods. Keep on writing, it's very therapeutic,' encouraged Hilda.

'But, in a way, my sister's death has also ended my own life. I never want to smile or experience any happiness ever again. It's totally destroyed me,' Autumn said. She felt comfortable sharing her real feelings, the things she would normally conceal.

'Autumn, dear. What was your sister's name?'

'Summer. And please don't make jokes about our names. And, yes, our parents were hippies.'

'Well, dear, if Summer could see you today, do you really think she would have wanted you to be in pain every single day? For the rest of your life? And simply to prove to everybody how much you loved her?' Hilda smiled warmly.

'Oh, heavens no! Summer would be very furious at me over this. She'd definitely be disappointed with my behaviour,' Autumn said, wiping her tears.

'Maybe the problem is that you're concentrating on the day of her death, rather than commemorating her life. How old was she when she died?'

'Eighteen,' said Autumn, gloomily.

'Okay, so Summer was alive for all of those eighteen wonderful and happy years. And you've decided to only concentrate on the day that she died. That doesn't make much sense, does it?' Hilda said confidently.

'You know, you're actually right. I had never, ever thought of it in that way before. I'd never thought of it like that until right now,' said Autumn, with a faint smile appearing on her face. Hilda hugged her. 'Thank you, Hilda. Thank you for your insight. I still have a long way to go but I think you truly have opened my eyes and given me a new outlook. I'm so grateful for that.'

As they finished hugging, the elevator suddenly began to move.

Leaving the building, it was clear that Hilda and Autumn were rather transformed by their encounter.

'It would be great if we could keep in touch,' said Autumn, typing Hilda's phone number into her phone. 'I'd love to hear about all your travel escapades, too.'

'Oh, that would be lovely, dear. And how did you know I was going to be travelling?' said Hilda, as she stared at the elevator one last time.

'Oh, only the fact that you've been holding plane tickets in your hands this whole time,' said Autumn, pointing to Hilda's paperwork. They laughed, waved and strolled away in different directions.

On her way home, Hilda decided to take a slight detour, to Pearl's house. 'Pearly, dear. Are you home?'

'Hilly! What a pleasant surprise! I wasn't expecting to see you today. I thought you'd be home, packing madly,' Pearl said, excitedly.

'I was, but I wanted to speak with you one last time before I head off. My phone was out of battery so I thought I'd talk to you, in the flesh,' explained Hilda.

'Okay, why don't you come in for a cuppa.' Pearly opened the door wide to let her sister in. Over tea and biscuits, the sisters reminisced about the good old days, as well as some deep and meaningful issues.

'I often have wondered what made you do everything you were told to do in life?' pondered Hilda.

'Well, I guess I had never enjoyed making decisions. In some ways, I was glad to have someone there to make them for me. Of course, now I do try to unearth what truly will make me happy. But I still find it a struggle making decisions and working out what my purpose is in the world,' said Pearl.

'True happiness is a bit of an illusion anyway. I mean, as long as you can do things you enjoy and are passionate about in your life, that is all you really need,' Hilda daydreamed as she sipped her tea.

'But, Hilly, aren't you at least curious about the possibility of experiencing love? Experiencing a relationship with your soul mate? Don't you want a companion in your life?'

'There are pros and cons to both situations, I guess. To being single and childless. To being married with children. There are good and bad aspects to everyone's life. I'm happy and confident with the path I chose and the decisions I've made.'

'Yes, you're right, Hilly. It's my responsibility to make my own decisions. Especially now that Walter has passed away. You know, he used to do all the finances and never told me anything about it. Now I have been forced to learn how to do everything. We cannot change others, only ourselves,' said Pearly, philosophically.

As Hilda left, she hugged her sister for a lot longer than she normally would. 'You do know that I love you, Pearly? I hope you know how much you mean to me and that I'm so happy you're in my world.'

'Yes, of course I do, Hilly. And despite how much

I think you're completely crazy at times, I also love you. Thanks for the visit, and I hope you enjoy the trip. I think you'll find, after you travel a bit, that your home town is just as fantastic as anywhere else in the world.'

'Thanks, Pearly, I will enjoy my travels. But I realise now that it's not the most important thing in my life,' said Hilda, as she wandered away into the distance, with a renewed perspective.

View from the Hill

Katharina Fares

Jack was on his way to his employer's house on the Peninsula with his great love. No, it wasn't a woman but a 1948 Jaguar Mark V, lovingly restored and polished into a gleaming work of art, at least in the eyes of its owner.

This car was the one luxury Jack allowed himself, although he had only paid for the restoration of it. His uncle, his mother's older brother, had left it to him in his will.

Jack had not valued it at first when he found it covered with grime and dust in a dilapidated shed on his uncle's country property. He only realised he had stumbled on a gem when his friend Owen was restoring vintage cars and seemed very eager to take it off his hands. However, when Owen understood Jack wouldn't sell it he was content to restore it for a reasonable amount of money.

Money was something Jack never had in abundance. Although he was a well-known investigative journalist and earned more than many of his colleagues, he spent most of it after each of his very dangerous assignments. In whatever corner of the globe he was, he stayed on for a while to get to know the people in a more peaceful environment—if there was such a spot—and told himself he needed to unwind and restore his energies and enthusiasm.

Now he wanted to settle down. He owed it to his mother to stay put, at least for a while until she had recovered from the accident. He would have to give up what he loved doing, but he needed a steady income. If money got really tight, Jack thought, he could sell the car.

It was hard enough for his mother to accept that his father had been killed while she was driving the car. She blamed herself for the collision, which didn't help in restoring her physical health. The investigating police said it wouldn't have mattered who was driving. The truck that collided with their vehicle spun suddenly out of control and crossed to the opposite side of the road. No one could have foreseen it.

She knew all of this, but her thoughts raced in circles and always came back to the same irrational conclusion—she was to blame. She needed Jack's support. He couldn't possibly put her through another period of worry every time he went away on another assignment.

The invitation to one of his boss's private residences was a good sign. Perhaps he would get an inkling of his prospects. Of course nothing definite would be said in such an informal setting, but there must be a good reason to invite him for a weekend. Jack knew that Wendy, his editor, was on more familiar terms with James Black, but as far as he knew no other staff-member was.

He had trouble finding the residence. The large impressive building was hidden from the street by a row of tall trees. He discovered the number of the place on a huge open gate and followed the driveway up the hill, until he saw the house perched on top of a cliff.

His car was taken care of and he was ushered through a wide entrance into an oversized reception room with floor to ceiling windows allowing a 180-degree view of sky and sea.

James Black and his wife, Sophie, welcomed him cordially and introduced him as some kind of a *Wunderkind* to a dozen or so guests who were already enjoying the drinks offered by waiters dressed in black and white.

'Nice to see you here, Jack,' said Wendy after they moved over to the windows.

'You too, Wendy.'

'I guessed you would be summoned, sooner or later.'

'What about you?'

'I was sounded out a long time ago. The powers above know where I stand. Listen carefully to every one tonight and Jack. Be careful of what you say.'

'Are you serious?'

'See for yourself,' Wendy said, as she raised her eyebrows and walked away.

What has gotten into Wendy? I'm sure she is mocking me, Jack thought, oblivious to the view of the ocean in front of him. But an uneasy feeling crept into him. Did he think he deserved to be invited to the highest echelons of society because of his merits, he asked himself, sarcastically?

When the murmur of soft conversations stopped he turned and saw James Black introducing a young woman to the group of people nearest to him. 'Cassy, my daughter,' he said.

'Cassandra, pleased to meet you.'

What was it that made people stare at her? Jack wondered. She wasn't conventionally beautiful, but had a tall and willowy figure, a very fair complexion and striking blue eyes. Her light-blonde hair was probably her natural colour.

It was Wendy who introduced her to Jack when James was monopolized by one of the other guests. The two women seemed to know each other well.

'Isn't it beautiful? It stops your heart,' Cassandra said, drawing their attention to the crimson and purple coloured clouds and the fiery ball of the sun sinking into the ocean. 'I see the commander has mobilized his troops,' she added.

'You are very suspicious,' Wendy replied.

'Perhaps you should be too. The tall man with the mop of grey hair is Harry Clark, an American multi-millionaire who has a significant number of shares in Dad's paper and also in an Australian television network. You must both know Leo Morel. He's the Australian CEO of a French multi-national company, which has investments in transport and energy production in many countries. They're looking for new investment opportunities.'

Jack's curiosity was raised. 'Did your father tell you this?'

'Of course not. He doesn't think women are interested, nor should they be according to him, in economic issues or any other issues. It doesn't apply to you, Wendy. I overheard him talking to Mother, giving her instructions to keep the wives out of the way.'

James Black came over and put his arm around Jack's shoulder. 'We are looking at some exciting possibilities for wealth creation for our country. You,

Jack, are the right man to investigate and report on the benefits to our economy.'

'Thanks for your confidence, Mr Black,' Jack said, thinking, such an assignment would be very different from the investigations he had done in the past.

'Cassy, please show the women our garden before it gets dark. No, not you Wendy. Could you come with us?' he said, pointing to the group of men in the middle of the room.

The women followed Sophie and Cassandra out of the room. There were five men left behind but only Harry Clark was talking. The four others were grouped around him listening respectfully to his animated explanations.

Jack quickly considered who was present. Apart from the CEO of the French company, there was Ben Smith from the Federal Department of the Environment. He had heard of him before but couldn't place Oliver Turner and Max Evans, the two younger men. It took him only a few seconds to understand Harry Clark was talking about the future of coal seam gas mining. Now I know where Cassandra is coming from, he thought. Clever girl.

'We will go strictly through the proper channels and apply for a referral and seek approval from the Federal Government,' Harry Clark said, looking at Ben Smith. Then he directed his steely gaze to Oliver Turner. 'On the local level we will provide a plan to the Department of Trade and Investment, outlining the benefits to the Australian economy and will cooperate fully with the Environment Protection Authority.'

'I doubt if the Department of Primary Industries and the Office of Water are as keen on such a proposal as the Department of Trade and Investment.' Cassandra's remark was met with startled faces. No one had noticed her coming back in. ‘After all this is a very invasive process and requires vast areas of fertile agricultural land.’

‘This is not an issue. Mining companies will pay adequate compensation to the affected landowners,’ Leo Morel said haughtily.

‘I am sure the landowners understanding of adequate will be very different from that of the mighty mining companies. I am also sure who will win if it comes to a disagreement,’ said Cassandra. ‘But the main threat to our environment is the contamination of water, of ground water and of our rivers.’

‘Cassy!’

‘James, let the child give us her opinion,’ Harry Clark said jovially.

Jack could see Max Evans waiting for an opening. ‘We have carried out extensive testing of drilling processes and investigated negative effects on the environment, and I can assure you, they are of no consequence compared to the economic benefits.’

‘I’d like to know who paid for the extensive testing.’

‘Young lady,’ Max Evans said sharply. ‘I resent your insinuation.’

‘Your process requires tens of thousands of drillings over vast areas of arable land. No one can guarantee there won’t be accidents from time to time. This will result in ground water contamination and many other kinds of pollution,’ Cassandra said heatedly.

Leo Morel rolled his eyes, ‘Here we have a little eco-warrior.’

‘My dear child, don’t listen to scare-mongering,’ Harry Clark said in a patronising tone, patting Cassandra’s shoulder.

James Black grabbed the arm of his daughter. Jack saw his knuckles turning white, but Cassandra ignored her father and said passionately, ‘It is all right for you people to dismiss any concerns. You will be dead when the consequences of your actions appear, but our generation will have to live in a world yours has destroyed.’

Wendy looked at Jack as if to say, I warned you.

The women came in from the garden and Sophie Black asked her guests to come with her into the dining room. Cassandra stared at Jack and followed her mother.

When everyone was seated, an exquisite meal diverted men and women to other less controversial topics. Nothing more was said about the purpose of this informal gathering. In fact, the rest of the evening was so pleasant and entertaining, one could have thought the heated exchanges ever took place.

Before Jack settled down for the night in a small but expensively furnished room with its own ensuite, he looked out of the window. It was too dark to see the ocean far below, but the brilliance of the stars lighting up the sky more than made up for it.

In the warmth of his bed the events of the evening rolled past his inner eye many times and each time came back to Cassandra. What an unusual girl she was. He finally drifted into a restless sleep, disturbed by a recurring dream.

He dreamed he left the house and wandered around a wooded area. There were many tall trees but also dense undergrowth. It was dark and difficult to move ahead. A voice called from a distance, ‘Jack, come with me.’ He saw a shadowy figure and asked, ‘Who are you?’

‘I am Mephistopheles. Come with me.’ As the figure came nearer he recognised the face of James Black. ‘Come with me to the top of the hill and look down at the riches of this world. I will give them to you if you support me. I will surround you with treasures if you stay on my side.'

Jack saw outstretched arms coming nearer and nearer to him. James Black loomed over him. 'Don't be a fool, Jack. You are talented, professional and tough. Your reports will convince any opponent of our plans. Think about your future.'

'Jack, Jack, look at me.' It was Cassandra's voice echoing from far below. Jack stepped forward and looked down from the hill to the sea. A slight shape, illuminated by silvery moonlight floated over the water, calling, 'Jack, Jack, stay true to yourself.'

Circles

Katharina Fares

Continuous line
no beginning or end
a symbol of love
of lover or friend

Children form a circle
through joining of hands
happily singing
moving in innocent dance

A circle of friends is wise to acquire
their gifts and talents good to admire

Some go through life in circles
around and around
to repeating dilemmas
with strong ties bound

Circular arguments never end

causing rifts in relationships
hard to mend

Vicious circle
consisting of severe actions
driven to continuity
by intensifying reactions

The tiger tempted
to jump through a circle of fire
conquers his fear
driven by submission and desire

Magic has claimed
the circle's powers
to keep evil in or out of it
in particular hours

Dervishes whirl
in a circle of meditation
reciting divine phrases
as rhythmical invocations

Crop circles burnt
permanently into the ground
all over the world
are searched for and found

Encircling Jupiter's orbit
disturbing thoughts
to be fearful and morbid
gigantic comet
broken up star matter
destined to collide
explode and shatter

Life and death
death and life
circles divine
the essence of creation
these circles enshrine

Laughter Needs No Translation

Sakuntala Gananathan

Kathryn was relating her ordeal to young Maria and her governess, who had come to visit her. 'On the second day, we crossed the French border. Around noon that day we reached a village, which I learned was Augustan. Atop a mountain, there was the steeple of a church silhouetted against a near-white sky. The vista across the valley was green and peaceful with occasional cottages dotting it, while herds of sheep grazed to their hearts' content. The very sight of the countryside was a balm to my sore heart, and I prayed I could bury my troubles in that place.

'In less than an hour we sighted a house with a tiled roof and smoke looping from a chimney. As though they had been alerted to my arrival, an old couple stood outside with broad smiles, and my anguish vanished upon seeing their cheerful faces. I said to them, "I shall relate to you the fiasco by and by, but first I must have my baby." The woman repeated, "Baby?" and looked at the bundle in my arms. She must have thought me odd, with my clothes daubed with mud and my feet lost in a large pair of shoes I had found in the wagon. Speaking in a mixture of French and another dialect, she insisted I have a bath before she would give me a hearing.

'It took me a while to get rid of the grime and dirt. After putting on a fresh set of clothes that my hostess gave me, I came out. There was a simple dinner of brown bread, cheese, and a jar of honey on the kitchen table. "And a jug of milk to wash it down with," the woman said, trying to humour me. Every sentence from her was preceded by a chuckle, and her light green eyes twinkled with mirth.

'I was in no mood to smile. "I want my baby, my own. This instant!" I noted with satisfaction that she stopped grinning. "We've been instructed to look after you both," said the man. "I am Max, and my wife is Greta." He had a burly physique, despite his age, and a head of silver-grey hair. His hooded eyes gave one the impression that he was half asleep. "Enough! She is not mine. There's been a mix-up, and you have to help me contact your masters to restore my child, whom I have not seen since the day of birth."

'Greta stared at me mournfully. "Oh, how terrible for you! We are greatly saddened to hear this, but we are unable to help you. We have never seen the owner of this house." In a moment, her smile returned, much to my disgust. "Once a month, a courier calls with money for our expenses and news of our next guests, whom we have to take care of until they think it fit to leave this place."

'Max intervened, "Yesterday a messenger arrived with a note from our master informing us that a young lady and her baby would be living with us indefinitely."

'I said in defiance, "It's not true. I have no idea who this little girl is, and I have come to take mine."

'Max ignored my plea. "Please inform your guest," he read the note with great solemnity, "that she will be endowed with an attractive annuity, which her benefactor is sure she will not refuse. She can stay as long as she wants to."

'By now I had become hysterical and went on repeating, "I want my baby!" Shaking his head at my outburst, he continued reading. "In the interest of her own safety, it is best that she live under an assumed name." He folded the paper with care and put it away.

'I tried to instil in the couple the urgency of the matter, but they were so overjoyed at the sight of the infant girl that all my entreaties fell on deaf ears. By now, I had a suspicion that they were deliberately ignoring my request. Were they in the service of my detractors? Unable to curb my grief, I let out a howl that would have echoed down the valley and across the mountains. Slowly, it dawned upon me that it wouldn't be easy for me to reunite with my baby. I realised to my horror that it was no mix-up but rather abduction, cruelly executed.'

Kathryn reached for Maria's hand. 'Although my pain was immeasurable, I found solace in seeing to your needs. In a world of treachery and deceit, you and I had only each other to comfort and to live for. I shed tears for your mother, but if she had appeared before me and asked me to return you, would I have complied with her request? Perhaps yes, only if she would have returned mine.'

'What if my mother had no knowledge of your baby but insisted she wanted me back? Would you have readily obliged my mother?'

'Not wanting another mother to suffer a fate like

mine, I would have given you away, though not readily, as you put it. All these fears would haunt me at night, and I would cry myself to sleep. Each time I heard a carriage clattering in the neighbourhood I would run out, expecting to see my beloved. As the noise of the wheels came louder and louder, my hopes would soar higher and higher, and when the sound receded in the distance, my heart would refuse to beat.'

'We lived there for about a year, and with each passing month my sorrow seemed to abate. I kept myself busy, helping Greta in the kitchen. She was a good cook and we traded recipes.

'Early one morning, I reached for you in the crib that Max had made and found you missing. Thinking Greta might have taken you to let me sleep longer, I came out to join them in the garden. When I approached them, fear and sadness were written on their faces. A feeling of dread overcame me when Max gave me a heavily sealed cover, which I slit open with trembling hands. It was unsigned but had the same fragrance—the same stink that I recalled from that ill-fated night. It made me nauseous, but I forced myself to read. "The girl will soon be in the safe care of a lady of great charm and diligence ..."

'A terrible sense of desolation overpowered me. I cried until there were no more tears to shed, because I had become very attached to you in the short period we were together. Furthermore, you were my only hope. With you in my care, there was every chance I would meet mine. My link with my past was now destroyed forever. I read the words again, "...in the safe care of a lady of great charm and diligence ..."

'Charm and diligence indeed! I sneered at the implication. Even if I were lacking in charm, need I be endowed with diligence to take care of you? Hadn't I proven myself more than capable after all the tribulations you and I had undergone together?

'The note continued. "Danger will befall you both if she is with you. Should you divulge this secret to anyone, you will regret the day you gave birth to your own, who is being held as ransom to buy your silence. Your child will be restored to you in good time, and, meanwhile, you will be well provided for as long as you are alive. Stay incognito." Thus, I lost both children within a year of each other.'

Kathryn fell silent, unable to continue.

'Please go on, Madame,' urged Maria after a long pause.

'Your abduction left me deeply grieved and I prayed that you would be joined with your parents at the earliest possible moment. I had to make peace with myself that my baby was alive, though held in captivity.

'In all these years, I haven't divulged my heartbreak to anyone in France, not even to my bosom friend Elise, from whom I was separated that miserable night up until a few months ago. I have lived in hope of joining my child, but that never came to pass. Instead, I've been a fugitive, hunted for more than a decade, assuming different names, and all my efforts to discover my beloved have come to naught.'

Time appeared to have stopped in the drawing room. The silence that shrouded them was broken with the neighing of horses in the courtyard.

'I can well understand what anguish you have endured, Madame,' the governess said, rising from her seat. She appeared anxious to leave.

'I hope and pray those responsible for this ghastly crime are punished suitably,' said Maria, her eyes shining with anger. She looked at Kathryn with greater respect than when she had first entered the room. They had both started on a journey of uncertainty and grief. But while she had been taken care of by a person who claimed to be her great aunt, Madame had had to live in perpetual fear for herself and her child. Maria waited till she regained her composure and asked softly, 'What about my parents? Are they living?'

Kathryn remained silent.

Maria had to return before anybody noticed her absence. All of a sudden she appeared to have lost her innocent, carefree disposition. *And here I am mulling over the threadbare dress that my surrogate mother is wearing.* A feeling of deep sorrow made her kneel before Kathryn. 'Please forgive me for not fully valuing your role when I came in. I'm now the wiser, stripped of all false airs with which I have been brought up.' After a pause the girl repeated her question. 'Can't you help me meet with my parents?'

'Well, I can make discreet enquiries about them so you can join them. All that my informant gave me was the location of an intermediary through whom I was able to arrange for this meeting. To be candid, I was eager to meet with you, for I have long thought of you as my own. It has been a double tragedy for me.' Kathryn embraced the girl and kissed her with affection.

'But do promise me you will leave no stone unturned till you find my parents.'

Seeing Maria's grief-stricken face, Kathryn embraced and her and said, 'I promise.'

'*Merci*. Please inform them my name is Anne-Marie … Maria for short.' She wished them both au revoir and left the room. The governess gave Kathryn a nod and followed her.

The ladies stood at the window, watching the

carriage move slowly down the driveway.

'I have sometimes felt as though I delivered twins and that fate willed both be torn from my aching arms. I have a strong feeling that one has visited me today.'

'I would agree with you,' said Elise, 'had I not been there all through your labour, praying I could share your pain. What if the midwife had, without your knowledge and mine, concealed the second delivery that was the girl?'

'That's bordering on the impossible,' said Kathryn, laughing. 'You haven't outgrown your youthful way of analysing a problem.'

'It sure is absurd, but my hunch feels so strong after meeting Maria—on sensing your reaction when she made her entrance, I wondered whether I had got the picture wrong: that yours was a girl and not a boy.'

'I wish it were so.' Kathryn sounded exhausted. 'My search would come to a happy end had it been Maria,' she said, biting her lip.

'You have much to reveal to me, Kathy,' Elise said, taking up a salmon pink gown to sew. 'Tell me where you've been all these years. I felt terrible that I was unaware of your misery. I hope you didn't continue living with the couple in Augustan after the little girl was abducted.'

'Well, I was afraid to live there, although they swore that they had no hand in the kidnapping. I couldn't trust them anymore. I had a suspicion that Greta's perpetual laughter was only a cover-up for their involvement with their employer, but I was discreet enough not to convey my distrust. I had to make my escape from there, but I had no resources to fall back on except for the monies that the author of the letter had dispatched to me. I was, however, determined not to ever touch a franc of the foul money.

'In hindsight, I regret I refused the money, and my false pride has cost me a decade,' Kathryn said, wringing her hands helplessly. 'Had I accepted the annuity, it would have served me as an umbilical cord to reach my son. Nothing sensible entered my head at that time. It was all a muddle … a strange land and strange people speaking a guttural dialect—a completely new world.

'On one occasion, Max and Greta planned to visit their daughter in Rozelle and invited me to join them. They said the place was near the French border and that the people spoke German as well as French. I was glad there was every chance for me to get back to Paris from there. But when I heard …' Kathryn stopped speaking upon seeing Simon at the door.

'Madame, please excuse me.'

'Yes, what is it?' Elise asked brusquely. She read the note he gave her and rose from her seat. 'Kathy, you'll have to manage without me for a week or more as I need to attend to an urgent order. Could you please leave this gown in my sewing basket? And Simon, have you cleaned my pistol? Check to see whether it's loaded.'

'Yes, Madame, cleaned and loaded,' he whispered in her ear, as though Mademoiselle Kathryn shouldn't be let in on the secret.

After he left, Elise told her that she carried the firearm to protect herself while travelling. 'It's my shadow. My chaperone.'

Kathryn didn't seem to hear Elise speak. Instead she seemed to hear Max repeat his invitation to her in Augustan. She thought Max was joking when he asked her to mount a donkey. And when she learned that the animal would lumber along a narrow ledge bordering a steep mountain, she squatted on the ground and refused to move. She was certain that her end was near. *Now what! Not enough they had aided the kidnappers, they want to do away with me as well.* 'Isn't there any other way to reach your daughter's house?'

Tugging at his moustache, Max said, 'Well, we can take the wagon on flat ground and skirt the mountain ranges. It will then take us a little more than a month to arrive at Stella's home.'

'Can I not walk behind the animal?' Even as she spoke, Kathryn knew she had to mutely follow the mule keeper, as would her donkey. *With Greta behind me, it's just child's play for her to feed me to the yawning below* she thought. With a grim set of her jaw, she mounted the mule.

Her heart was in her mouth for the next few hours. On one side was the steep incline of rugged cliffs and on the other side was a bottomless gorge. One false move by the animal and both would go hurtling down to their deaths. While she trembled at the thought, she was amazed to find herds of mountain goats standing upright and happily grazing on grassy patches.

The travellers were now at the mercy of the donkeys bearing their weight, and Max looked comical with his stirrups stretched out so that his shoes wouldn't rake up the gravel. At short intervals his keeper halted the creature to let Max rest his numb limbs on solid ground, and the second keeper had the unpleasant task of pacifying Kathryn and the animal each time the exchange took place with Max.

Soon the abyss evened out slightly, and there was now a valley covered with stretches of edelweiss and hyacinth. It was like a giant carpet. On the hills across the great divide was a forest of elm and silver birch.

Kathryn had no more cause to distrust her

companions, and she looked over her shoulder to wave at Greta. 'You're right, there's nothing to be afraid of anymore.'

As though to dampen Kathryn's enthusiasm, her donkey gave a jerk so violent that she shut her eyes and said her prayers until they reached flat terrain.

The path now merged into a well-trodden road, which branched out to settlements belonging to shepherds. After an hour or so, they arrived at a township of neatly laid out houses, with rows of azaleas flanking vegetable patches. Max alighted from his mare but let the ladies continue their ride.

The locals were simply dressed—men in breeches and dark tunics and women in skirts and white blouses colourfully embroidered. They stopped to greet the newcomers with a smile or passed them with a nod.

Stella was overjoyed to see her parents. 'It's such a wonderful surprise,' she said, kissing them. She was a tall woman with close-set eyes, the colour of honey, and long, golden hair. Greta made the introductions, and the daughter shook hands with her guest. She put away their baggage and led them to the kitchen at the rear. It was large and airy with spice containers neatly stacked on wooden shelves alongside one wall. They sat around a large oak table, on the centre of which were bottles of sauces of various colours and sizes. Stella treated them to apple strudel and coffee with cream.

The family switched over to their native dialect, and although Kathryn couldn't follow what they spoke, she had a suspicion it was about her reluctance to get on the mule. They had a hearty laugh at her expense, and she, too, joined in the mirth. *It's true,* she thought happily, *that laughter needs no translation.*

After hearing from her father about Kathryn's

ordeal, Stella asked her, 'Why not live with us here?' Much to Kathryn's delight, she spoke French, grammatically flawless but with a broad accent.

Presently her husband Dane joined them. He had a blond head of hair on his tall frame, and though sallow faced, he had a cheerful disposition. Dane and Stella were theatre actors and invited Kathryn to join their troupe.

'Well, I'm not keen on acting,' said Kathryn, her cheeks turning a dark pink. She seemed to hear her aunt screaming, 'Scandalous! Women on stage! Unheard of!'

'If you can help me get a job … say as governess …"

Stella grunted before she finished speaking. 'Governess? Not for children here. We are uniformly middle-class and have no need for an idle tutor living off our hard-earned bread.' Seeing Kathryn's drawn face, she added on a softer note, 'Papa briefed me of your misery. Rest assured. There's no likelihood of your detractors coming to this side of the mountains, to reach which one has to humour a donkey.'

'But I need to fend for myself. I can't live off charity!'

'What you need is a good job,' said Stella, chopping meat and turnip for a stew. 'What better way than taking to acting? We are like a close-knit family, similar to gypsies and circus troupes, except that we have pitched our tent here permanently.' She gave her one of Greta's smiles and added, 'It's the people who travel to see us.'

Kathryn had found an ally in Stella and was glad she had made the trip. She felt guilty for having mistrusted the old couple, but found it odd that Stella's smile was so engaging, unlike her mother's.

On the Side of a Hill

S.C. Karakaltsas

The sun is low on the horizon when we stroll arm in arm around the large park. A mob of roos stand tall, staring long and hard at us, ears twitching, dropping their heads to eat only after we're at a distance. We stop to take in the view. The bay spreads out before us shimmering flat except in the wake of an ocean liner, which sails in slow motion toward the Heads.

We pass a silent group of women, arms arched in Tai Chi moves. A flock of rosellas take flight. We stop to listen to rustling in the bushes nearby, hoping for a glimpse of something, which never reveals itself.

'The sign said this way,' my husband announces.

But all we find is another lookout and more staring roos. The ocean liner edges closer to the Heads.

An old, dusty path leads us to a lake surrounded by reeds and a fence.

'Look,' he says. 'There's another sign. Sculptures this way.'

My enthusiasm and energy is waning as we climb another hill. I'm at the point where I want to go back, but we find ourselves in a picnic area, desolate except for a young couple on a chequered picnic rug.

'What a good idea,' I say. 'Why didn't we think of doing that?'

'Yeah,' he says, still searching for the sculptures.

'They're probably celebrating their wedding anniversary.'

He glances at the couple before scanning the slope ahead.

'Nah. It's a first date for sure.'

By now we've moved on and are on a path above the couple and can see what they see. The ocean liner is long gone. The sea is flat, its colour a pale blue.

'No, it's not. Look, they've got champagne and glasses and a picnic basket. She's not dressed up for a first date. Why don't we just sit on the grass and watch the sunset too? Let's forget about the sculptures. They're obviously not around here. I'm tired.'

'Where's the map? I reckon we're close.'

I rummage in my pocket, pull out the map and hand it to him. He studies it.

'I bet he's surprised her. They've been married a couple of years and he's gone to all that effort,' I say. I imagine the man getting everything ready and telling his wife they're going for a drive. She would have smiled and kissed him.

I stare at the couple instead of the view. 'You'd never think about doing something like that for me.' The thought sneaks out and hangs between us. We walk on.

'What's that over there? Just past the pink barked gum. I think that must be one. See?' He points into the bush. 'They're arguing anyway.'

I swing my head back to gawk at the couple.

'Don't look!' he says. 'Wow.'

My head swivels back to face the large sculpture ahead of us.

'My god. This is magnificent,' he says, studying the rusted, twists of metal pretending to be art. 'Your sister is really talented.'

'How do you know they're arguing?'

'I heard them. Don't you think this piece is great? Look how the light reflects on the metal.'

'What did you hear?'

His excitement drops and he sighs. 'He told her to stop being paranoid. You should be checking out your sister's art. This is important.'

I hear raised voices drifting away into the other direction.

'Stand against this tree and kiss me so I can see what's going on.'

'I'm not going to do that. That's so obvious.'

'Too scared to snog in public now?' I tease. 'C'mon. At least stand there so I can face you and see what's going on behind you.'

He complies but grumbles, 'You're such a busy body.'

Looking over his shoulder, I brush a leaf from his hair.

'Gee, I think you're right. He's standing. He's pacing backwards and forwards.'

He touches my shoulders and moves me aside. 'There's another one. C'mon. Let's go.'

'But don't you want to know what's going on?'

He grabs me around my shoulders pulling me into him.

'No. And neither should you. Stop spying on them. Now let's do what we set out to do.'

'But what if that girl's in trouble? Maybe we should stick around.'

'Now *you're* being paranoid. That's stupid. It's none of our business. She'll be fine. It seems to me you're chickening out.' He grabs my hand and pulls me along. I know he's right but I don't want to go on. I turn for another look. The man is waving his arms as if in explanation. The woman, seated on the blanket, pulls her knees up under her.

We round the bend. More roos and a sculpture of a large shiny silver gnome.

I can't resist turning my head one more time, but the couple are no longer in sight. I'm torn. I want to see them and the fading view rather than face what I know is before me. He lets go of my hand and wanders ahead.

'There's meant to be another one further along the track,' he calls out.

I stare at the gnome, but I'm thinking about the couple. I'm agitated. My sister's sculpture disturbs me.

'You coming?' he calls out.

'Yeah.' I jog to catch up and gasp. 'Oh my god,' is all I can say.

There it is: a skeleton of a small child lying in the bush. The title says, 'Lost'. The sculpture takes my breath away. My chest thumps and my hands sweat. For the first time in twenty years tears slide down my cheeks. I bury my head into my husband's shoulder and sob, the arguing couple and their woes replaced by a volcano of erupted grief. Slumped in his arms I'm comforted by my husband's smell and familiarity. After a while I pull away to stare again at the art piece.

'You alright?' he asks softly.

I nod and sniff. 'It's more confronting than I expected.'

'You said you were ready.'

I wipe my nose with the back of my hand. 'I thought I was.'

He kisses me and holds me close. We stand together staring at it in the fading light.

'I thought I could handle it. All those years of counselling. Maybe I'll never get over it. Now that I've seen this I don't know how my sister had the guts to do it.'

'Maybe it's her way of dealing with the grief of losing her child.'

I twist away to run up to the path. He catches up and we slow to a walk.

'I should have been watching out for her,' I say. I try to control the tears but they come in a flood. 'And…

and none of us even noticed she was gone.'

'You're being too hard on yourself. It was a long time ago. You were only a young girl.'

He was right, but it didn't make me feel any better.

'If only I'd checked on her.'

'It wasn't your responsibility.'

'You don't understand.' I stare into my trusting husband's eyes and put both my hands on his arms. I have to tell him everything. 'I promised my sister I'd check on her. That I was going to the bathroom, that I would go past her tent and look in.' I wipe away my tears and gulp. 'But I didn't check on her. I went behind the camping ground kitchen and smoked a joint with one of the boys.' I'd finally said what I'd never said to anyone. What I'd tucked away. I wait for my husband to say something, but there's only sympathy and love in his eyes.

It's then it hits me; I'd always had an excuse and now I know why. 'I can't be trusted with kids,' I blurt. 'That's why … why we've never had any.'

I let him go and turn away, don't want to see his face or his disappointment. I'd failed us both. The realisation of why we had no children, the excuses and the lies, were out.

'I never told anyone … until now.' I face him. 'I'm really sorry.'

He blinks and I can see he's trying to take it all in. Red marks multiplying across his neck show me his stress. I'm scared of what he'll do, what he'll say. I don't know if I can bare it.

'It's alright,' is all he says. 'It's going to be alright.'

I wipe my eyes again and look into his face. But I can't make out what he's thinking.

'Do you want to go home now?' he asks softly.

I nod and sniff back the snot to stop it sliding down

my throat. We walk on in silence for a while, thoughts and feelings pummelling my core. We reach the front gate of our rented cottage.

'It's time,' I say. 'It's time I faced my sister again. Tell her what I did and that I'm sorry.'

He kisses me and nods.

A swathe of orange cloud smears itself across the sky hiding the sinking sun.

'It's the right thing to do,' he whispers.

A View from the Hill

Marlene Laurent

Every time our car bumped along the dirt track to my uncle's farm my heart would beat faster and faster. Each gate we opened along the road meant we were getting closer to his property.

From the top of the steep hill we descended with trepidation, trying to avoid the potholes gouged out by years of erosion and the latest rainfall. The view from the hill was breathtaking. I saw the farmhouse that I had visited in the past with my mother, nestled in a lush green valley. The hill opposite the house was studded with gum trees. On this visit I was going to live here. As a five year old I would live in the world of the farmer and his wife, my aunt and uncle. I'd see their isolation, their challenges and a way of life completely different from that of the city I came from.

Their farmhouse, nestled in the valley of the Little River, became our home. To be sent away at the age of five would have a lasting impact on my life. Despite this, farm life was a novelty for my sister and me. So although we had moments of being homesick we loved it.

We fell out of bed next morning as my sister and I waited for the mail to arrive. With it came large loaves of fresh bread and maybe a letter from home, as well as the next batch of school lessons. As Uncle Jim saddled up the mare, my sister and I begged to be allowed to ride to collect the mail bag from the letter box, a half-gallon drum mounted on a gum tree that was situated at the corner of the dirt track that led into the first paddock of the farm. Alas, Aunty Rose wouldn't allow us to ride with him. The responsibility of looking after us weighed heavily on her. It wasn't until months later that I understood her cautious approach to allowing us to participate in farm life.

When Jim returned from his short ride to the letter box my sister and I watched with bated breath as he emptied the contents of the sac onto the floor in the kitchen. There was always a letter from Mum, matter of fact in nature, but never failing to assure us that she missed and loved us.

Each school morning the radio crackled into action with the familiar music and the teacher's voices, instructing us how to complete our lessons. The schoolroom was our dining room where we'd listen to and complete our lessons under the watchful eye of Aunty Rose. As it was my first year of schooling it didn't seem unusual to be educated by radio of the air. For my sister it was a different story. She was five years older than me and missed her friends. With a five-year gap, I guess I wasn't much company for her. We completed our lessons in double quick time knowing we would be allowed to go out and spend the rest of the day on the farm.

One evening Rose and Jim were sitting by the fire talking as it crackled and sent shadows dancing on the wall. We had just finished reciting the Rosary and Litany of the Saints and had been put to bed. Their voices were lowered, and I had to lie very still to hear their conversation from the room next door to our bedroom.

'Mary would be thirteen today,' my aunt whispered in a sad voice.

'Yes,' replied Jim. 'If only we had bought a new cot or been happy with the old one. Why did we paint it?' Then silence reigned.

My brain was racing, calculating that it wasn't my birthday and I didn't remember being in a cot on the farm. Eventually I drifted off to sleep.

The farm provided us with meat, milk, cream and butter. Every now and then we had chicken and, of course, homegrown fruit and vegetables. Our staple diet was lamb. My sister enjoyed eating the brains, while I liked the kidneys and black pudding. My aunt would buy flour, sugar, tea and other additives to spice up her cooking when we went into town.

We all knew when it was time to kill the sheep because my uncle would choose a chubby lamb and put it in the pen for a few days prior to slaughter. I always wanted to leave the gate open so it could escape death, but I never did. It was expected of us that we would toughen up on the farm. When it was time he would look around as he took a knife from the dairy and say, 'Can't do this on my own. Who is going to help me?' Invariably, I would volunteer, feeling a responsibility to contribute. There was a pulley, which was used to hoist the sheep up into the air once it had been killed. As I punched the skin off I could feel the warmth of skin under the wool coat. My uncle would sling the sheep's carcass over his shoulder after putting it into a cotton bag.

The dairy was adjacent to the old house where Grandma and Grandpa had lived. My eyes took time to adjust to the dimness. But the coolness of the place was a joy in the heat of the burning summer days. It was here we would hang the sheep and leave it to cure for a week until it was ready to eat.

The highlight of each month was a drive to Bathurst for supplies. On the way, we would pass through the many gates of the property. Each gate had its own personality. My gate was made of wood cut from a gum tree and was smooth, round and irregular in shape. I loved how the old thing was held together only by twisted wire. The rough and primitive way it had been made contrasted with the natural beauty of the wood. I would jump from the car and run to open it, avoiding the many cowpats, some fresh, some old. It creaked a welcome as if to say, 'So you're back.'

I would be careful to check for snakes, as they would come out to sunbake on hot days. The beauty of the Australian bush and the heralding of the seasons would see the yellow wattles bursting against the green leaves in spring, or the bush covered in a mantle of snow in winter. Both were wondrous sights to behold. Summer was dry and unforgiving.

Passing the local cemetery Rose and Jim would bless themselves and pray silently. Then we'd approach the swollen river and Jim would have to decide whether we could make it to the other side without being washed away. Sometimes the car would stall and we would be stranded. The river always dictated whether we could drive to Bathurst.

In September the sheep would be shorn. The shearing shed was a place of wonder. I was sitting on the fence by the shed, waiting to follow instructions about which gate to open, when Jim shouted, 'You ruddy coot!' (This was what he called the dog when it stuffed up.) 'Someone stop that sheep!'

Impulsively, I jumped into the race only to be trampled by the nervous runaway sheep. Jim laughed until his sides nearly split as I got up and dusted myself down. The only thing injured was my wounded pride.

As I stepped into the dimness of the shed the buzzing of the shearing machines, the shouting of instructions by the shearers and the bleating of the terrified and confused animals pervaded the busy atmosphere. The smell of the fleece and the sheep droppings were at first offensive, but soon became familiar.

The shearers were working at a frenetic pace as they were paid by the number of sheep shorn. Their reputation was at stake because whoever held the record for the most sheep per day was assured of work. There were four sets of shearing implements and so four sheep would be shorn in double quick time. There was always a race to see who could shear the most in a day. An overall tally was kept. Tar was applied to any cuts, and the fleece was thrown onto the table to be sorted. The bulk then went into a bale bag to be transported for sale. Sometimes I was allowed to label the bag, once the fleece had been pressed and sealed using a metal plate with my uncle's details on it. It read: Waterford Porter's Retreat.

Rose would bake up a storm for the shearers during the fortnight they worked at the farm. Cherry pie and cream was their favourite. At night they slept in the shearing shed. Uncouth language was the order of the day, and Rose would say we were not allowed in the shed with the shearers because of their bad language and manners, but Jim allowed us to join in so long as we didn't tell her, which, of course, we never did.

Jim showed me how to recognise the best wool. The quality was judged on how tight the wrinkles were and how greasy the wool felt. I used to keep samples of the wool that had fallen on the floor to take home to Melbourne. I kept it in a Cadbury chocolate tin I had in my wardrobe. My uncle's wool was first class and won many prizes. He kept meticulous records of which sheep had the best wool.

Christmas on the farm posed some challenges for Rose and Jim. They had no children, but they had to play Santa for us. During one of our trips to Bathurst, Rose took me to the toyshop. In the window was a doll. She asked me, 'Would you like Santa to bring you a doll for Christmas?' I looked at the doll for a minute or two, then turned to her and said, 'No. I want pink gum boots and a pop gun.' The look on her face said it all.

While she was decorating the Christmas tree, she assured my sister and me that Santa knew we were living with her and not at our own house in Melbourne. As Christmas drew closer, we counted down the days on the Advent calendar. We enjoyed doing this because the final twelve days before Christmas had a chocolate behind each window.

A lot of planning and preparation went into Christmas day lunch. The pig that had been purchased for the occasion was being kept on the neighbouring property ready for slaughtering. We rode across the river and up the steep slope through Kelly's empty property, to Neupers. The Neupers were our nearest neighbours. The property on the other side of the river had been empty ever since I had been visiting the farm. We had fun playing in the old house when we went there. We got to know the Neupers at the church when we went. I was given the task of removing the hairs from the pig by scraping them off with a saucepan. The pig was then shared between the two families.

Christmas Day began with a drive to the church. As the ute maneuvered its way up the dirt track my uncle stopped. Our mare was due to have a foal, and he wanted to check all was well. To his surprise and our delight he came back with the news that she'd given birth to a foal, and it was a female. We all fell from the ute to see her, and on the way to church we decided to name her Lady Noela.

As we drove past the little cemetery, my curiosity got the better of me and I asked Rose why she always looked so sad when we passed. Jim was driving, and he showed no emotion as Rose told us they had a little girl called Mary. She'd died when she was eighteen months old. She had chewed her cot, which had been painted with a lead based paint. Poisoning was the result. They hadn't been able to get her to the hospital in time to save her. We were silent for the remainder of the trip. The name Mary haunted me for the rest of my life.

The Claytons were our neighbours. They had settled on the neighbouring property in the late 1800s and not much had changed since then. Their life was simple.

The first time I rode in the ute with my uncle to visit Christie Clayton, I was fascinated. He lived in a primitive hut with dirt floor and mud brick walls. In those days he stood up tall and proud. 'Lovely to see you, Jim. And who may I ask is this?'

'This is my niece, Mary Marlene. She's from Melbourne.'

Christie had a puzzled look on his face as he responded in his slow drawl, 'Oh, I know, you're from way down south.'

'Yes,' I replied as I shook his outstretched hand. It was rough from outdoor work but his handshake was gentle.

His hut had no electricity or gas, so the warm glow of the fire was inviting. The smell of rabbit stew filled my nostrils as Jim and I sat on a stump log seat. Christie asked, 'Would you like a cup of tea?' He made it in a Billy Can using the boiling water from a large black kettle hanging over the fireplace. The chimney took up one wall of the house, as did the fire burning below it in the massive fireplace. He refilled the kettle from a barrel, which was filled by water from his roof via a piece of bark.

As I sat sipping the tea from a tin mug, we had a friendly chat. 'How is Mrs Conlon?' he asked respectfully.

'Busy baking cherry pies with cherries picked from your orchard,' I replied, remembering the delicious smell of them baking in her oven. His gentle green-grey eyes twinkled in delight at the thought of eating cherry pie topped with clotted cream. His shaggy eyebrows and ruffled hair, which had obviously been cut with the shears, were covered by his felt broad brimmed hat. He commented on the weather, being too wet or too dry, depending on the season. At shearing time the conversation would inevitably be about the wool, whether it was top quality or about how much it would fetch at the sales.

I loved to feel his bushy whiskers when he kissed me goodbye. 'Come again soon,' he would call in his eventually familiar drawl. I could feel his loneliness as he stood in the doorway (although there was no door on his hut) waving until we were out of sight. 'We will,' I would say quietly to myself. I think Christie loved me to visit just as much as I loved to visit him.

Twenty years later I returned. He hadn't seen me since I was fourteen, so I didn't know what to expect. I wanted him to meet my husband and my two-year-old daughter. Would he remember me or the wonderful times we had spent together? He must have been in his nineties. However, it was difficult to tell because to me he had always been old.

As he did all those years ago, he greeted us at the door. I introduced myself to him watching for a flicker of recognition. He responded in his Australian outback drawl. 'Mary Marlene, I remember you. You are the girl from way down south.'

I was flabbergasted and thrilled that he recognised me after all this time. As I had predicted, he launched into the story I knew so well and he had told me so many times. It was the story about how his mare had just delivered a foal and I went to see it. He had looked at me and said, 'What will I name the foal?' I had boldly replied, 'Mary Marlene, of course!' It was as if time had stood still. I treasured my last wonderful day on Christie's farm with him.

A letter had arrived from my mother informing Jim and Rose that she would be coming to take us home. Although we were young, we knew that we would be returning to our old life in the city. My mother was pregnant with my brother, and she had decided to stay with my father who was an alcoholic. I will always remember Rose standing at the front door of the house waving her hanky, which she used to mop her tears, until we vanished from view over the hill.

To our joy, we visited the farm every Christmas holiday and spent many happy times with my cousins from Sydney.

Years later when I returned as an adult the spring in the top paddock had dried up. It hadn't snowed for at least twenty years, and the river was a trickle of its former self. Even so the platypus family that lived in the river at the bottom of the paddock was still there.

Race to Notting Hill

Bala Mudaly

Port Phillip District 1853

Drays and carts were to race Mr Cobb's newly acquired Concord Coach, the first of its kind in Port Phillip Colony. The race was to be run from Oakleigh Village to Notting Hill. It had the blessing of Governor La Trobe himself as he hoped it would lift the spirits of the settlers who had fallen into hard times. Mr Swanson, a wealthy businessman, had pledged the grand sum of twenty guineas to whomever won the race.

The only rule was that vehicles that reached Oakleigh by nine o'clock that evening could enter the race. Many people took bets on which vehicle would win. Others said it was all too obvious that the coach would be a certain winner.

A large crowd gathered at the banks of the Yarro-Yarro on the first Sunday morning in January 1853 and gave the competing vehicles a rousing send off.

Arriving in Oakleigh Village

It was dark as a dunny at night when Grandpa's coach finally arrived in Oakleigh Village. Nanna, Martha and I hugged and kissed in great relief. What with the dust, sweaty heat and constant jolting on rough gravel, Nanna called the journey a hell run. Grandpa pulled on the reins while Nunga, his native helper and horse whisperer, spoke soothingly to the two horses. The coach slowed and finally stopped. I peered out the coach window and spotted flickers of lamp light. Voices could be heard. Uncle Lenny, who had ridden all the way on his horse Chomp Chomp, helped us three to get down. Nanna could barely stand, so Martha, her native helper, and I supported her on either side. It was so comforting to be standing again on solid ground. Confined for almost eight hours in the heat and dust of a January day had exhausted us. We were thirsty and desperate for a good feed, a good wash and hours of rest. As my eyes became accustomed to the dark, I noticed a few tents pitched in a small clearing near a line of mounds, each marked with a simple wooden cross. The place gave me the shivers.

'Are we to stay the night in a graveyard?' I whispered to Uncle Lenny, tugging at his coat hoping those buried there would not hear me.

'This is as safe a place as any, Pippa,' he assured me. 'Not likely to be attacked by natives or kangaroos for that matter. That there fire will burn through the night, and we'll be in the company of friendly folk.'

Looking out towards where Uncle Lenny was pointing, I noticed men seated near the tents smoking and drinking, a small pit fire lighting up their bearded faces.

Three large women hurried over to us holding

candles. 'Welcome, ladies. You must be with Mr Cobb? said the lead lady who introduced herself as Mrs Atkinson.

'Don't worry as we'll take good care of you all,' she lisped and spluttered, her mouth bereft of any teeth. 'Sadly though, our hospitality is quite modest.' Nanna thanked the women profusely.

After we had taken turns in the dunny, each of us savoured a good wash and, thereafter, bowls of steaming chicken broth, which brought on the yawns thick and fast. I was barely awake when I crawled into a tent pitched near the line of graves. Nanna lay on a swag next to me. Not even the mosquitos and other creatures that invaded the tent could disturb us. Uncle Lenny and Grandpa had the next tent, while Martha and Nunga preferred to sleep in the open close to the pit fire under a star-filled sky.

The insistent laugher of a kookaburra woke me. Nanna, however, was still tossing and turning in troubled sleep.

'Are you and Nanna awake, Pippa?' It was Uncle Lenny calling from outside our tent. 'The race starts soon.'

I hurried to tidy myself. Mrs Atkinson's helper brought me a dish of water and a cloth. All the while I worried about Nanna. As if she had read my mind, Mrs Atkinson stuck her head into the tent to check on us.

'Your Nanna's still asleep? I can tell she's an ill woman in need of much rest and healing. This is where she'll remain until tomorrow when I expect you'll return from Notting Hill, when this foolish race is done.' I felt so relieved Nanna was in good hands.

Grandpa was visibly irritated when Mrs Atkinson addressed him sternly. He promptly confided his anger to Uncle Lenny, Nanna's half-brother. 'Can you believe what that woman just said? A Concord Coach is no better than common drays and carts to transport women on such a hazardous track. Such a sentiment is quite outrageous, especially from a woman!' Realising how easily Grandpa's bloated pride tended to be bruised, Uncle Lenny listened without comment.

Having instructed Martha to stay back and care for Nanna, Grandpa turned to me. The moments silence seemed to last forever. I wrung my hands hunting for the right words with which to plead my case to go on the coach all the way to Notting Hill.

'Pippa, dear, it isn't proper for you to travel without female company,' said Grandpa.

'Surely Pippa is our responsibility, Mr Cobb,' intervened Uncle Lenny. 'We can't burden Mrs Atkinson unduly.' Grandpa continued chewing on the end of his unlit cigar.

'Please, Grandpa, I'll be no problem. Please! I so want to see you win the race. And I'll be the only woman there to tell people, from real experience, how comfortable coach travel is.'

That decided it for Grandpa. He smiled, clearly persuaded by the vision of his Concord Coach arriving in Notting Hill to wild cheers and merriment, and the competing drays nowhere to be seen. Uncle Lenny winked as he helped me into the coach and then handed me a basket of essentials, compliments of considerate Mrs Atkinson.

All Set To Go

The competitors assembled before Mr Atkinson, who was to adjudicate the race. From the vantage point of the coach window, I had the best view of everything. There were four men in all, including Grandpa. He was a tall, distinguished man in a top hat, black tailcoat and riding breeches.

'That's Mr Campbell next to Grandpa,' explained Uncle Lenny, who stood by the coach window holding his horse Chomp Chomp by the rein, while puffing on his pipe. 'Operates a transport business, he does. The race was actually his idea, Pippa. He's out to discredit Grandpa, who believes coaches will soon be the most popular transport in Port Phillip District.'

'I hope he doesn't win the race then,' I blurted.

'Then there is Mr Rodney the baker,' continued Uncle Lenny. 'And next to him is the man who calls himself Jefferson.'

'Oh! So his name's Mr Jefferson is it? The mad man who shot past Grandpa yesterday on the Damper Track from Melbourne, almost causing an accident?' It made me angry simply remembering the incident. The man still had no hat to protect himself from the fierce sun, having lost it when it fell into the creek while he was overtaking our Concord Coach. He looked weary now and out of place as if he hadn't slept or eaten for many days. I wondered who he really was and why he had entered the race. 'Could he be an escaped convict?' I asked. 'One can't be too careful!'

'Hush, not that loud, Pippa. True, the man's a stranger to us. Newly arrived in Melbourne, he says. But let not our fear and anger lead us to hasty conclusions.'

'Now, gentlemen, hear me out,' said Mr Atkinson, the husband of our caring host. An eager and excited crowd of adults and children had gathered in front of the line of graves. Nanna and Martha stood near Mrs Atkinson, their faces showing how worried they were for my safety.

'You'll likely find the track to Notting Hill more

challenging and treacherous than the run from Melbourne, what with stray animals, boulders and an occasional fallen tree,' Mr Atkinson continued. 'Look out to your own safety and respect your fellow competitors.'

Grandpa and the others nodded. Mr Atkinson would certainly be knowledgeable of the local terrain since he was in charge of the pound for stray animals at Scotchman's Creek.

'In conclusion,' said Mr Atkinson, 'may I add that anyone who cheats or intentionally endangers others will be disqualified from the race and reported to the colony's constabulary. I hope I make myself abundantly clear.' He looked fixedly in the direction of Mr Jefferson who, at that moment, seemed engrossed in his battered boots. 'I'll now ride ahead and wait your arrival in Notting Hill at Wilkinson's Grocery Store & Bakery. My good wife will start you off.' With that, Mr Atkinson mounted his horse and rode away. Uncle Lenny mounted Chomp Chomp in readiness to ride ahead of Grandpa and be his scout.

The Race

Mrs Atkinson raised the Union Jack in her right hand and waited until the competitors were seated in their vehicles with taut reins in hand. At the fall of the flag, the two drays, the baker's cart and the Concord Coach burst into motion, raising cheers, cat-calls and clouds of dust, which billowed over the spectators, scattering them coughing and spluttering. I was not spared either. The baker's cart, being the lightest, bolted ahead. Grandpa kept up a furious pace, with the other two drays close behind.

'You going well, Mr Cobb,' I heard Nunga say. 'Them drays lost far behind.'

'Yeah. Luck be with us, we'll be in Notting Hill before noon sipping beer. You mark my word.'

Uncle Lenny returned to advise Grandpa that the track ahead was dangerously narrow in parts with unexpected sharp bends. 'I'll ride behind you for a bit so as not to hinder your progress,' he said. Nunga urged his horses with soothing sounds. We made steady progress. The coach rushed on and on, over ruts and bumps and patches of loose gravel, dodging tree stumps and large rocks. The heat and dust made breathing quite difficult. I held on as best I could, and sang under my breath to keep me calm.

Suddenly, the world collapsed around us like we were hit by an earthquake. In a frightening second the coach lurched sideways and came to a violent stop throwing me onto the floor. Nunga screamed in alarm and Grandpa shouted, 'Oh, bugger me, oh, bugger me!'

I was dizzy and struggled to lift myself up, but couldn't do so as the vehicle was tilted to one side. My left elbow bled from a slight grazing. The next minute Uncle Lenny reached into the coach, eased me out and rested me gently on the dirt. I was dazed and unsure what had happened.

'There's been a little accident, Pippa. Nothing too serious for you to fret over. Grandpa and I are sorting it out. Close your eyes now and rest a little.'

I was just about dozing off when voices close by alerted me, and I sat up. Grandpa and Uncle Lenny were talking in low voices. They looked troubled. Grandpa's top hat was crumpled and there was dirt on his jacket. Nunga was close by in the shade of a tea tree carefully inspecting the two horses, which he had unhitched from the coach. His face and hands were covered in dirt, and his shirt was shredded at the side. I limped close to them. Grandpa put his arm around my shoulders and drew me close. 'I'm so relieved you're not seriously hurt, dear. I only wish I hadn't brought you along.'

A warm wind disturbed the tall gums making them creak and complain. I didn't feel well.

We all stood in shock looking about, taking in our misfortune. The coach had spun off the track and lay to one side. What shocked us was seeing the baker's cart nearby as well, badly damaged and blocking the track. It was still hitched to the horse, now crumpled and lifeless. An emaciated dead cow lay partly under the cart. Waves of frantic flies covered both dead animals. I became tearful and looked away.

'It's obvious what happened,' observed Uncle Lenny. 'The baker's cart ploughed into that wretched cow, a likely stray from Mr Atkinson's Pound. Mr Rodney then shot his wounded horse and took off.'

'I rounded this here blind bend at a great pace,' explained Grandpa, 'and hit right into the abandoned cart like colliding into a mountain face in fog. That infernal baker deserves to hang. Surely he could have warned us before fleeing.'

'In truth, I'm the guilty one, Mr Cobb,' moaned Uncle Lenny. 'As your eyes and ears, I should have stayed ahead of the coach and alerted you.'

The two drays caught up with us; the one belonging to the unpleasant Mr Jefferson and the other owned by Mr Campbell. Mr Campbell was appalled to see the coach stranded in the middle of the track in a calamitous state, so much so that he stopped his dray, dismounted and hastened over to enquire what had happened. Mr Jefferson, on the other hand, hesitated a moment, slowing his dray just enough to scan over us once, with eyes as dreary as an overcast winter's morning. Then he drove on in silence, carefully avoiding the coach, the baker's cart and the dead animals.

'You'll still stay in the race, Mr Cobb, won't you?' asked Mr Campbell, shaking his head in disbelief.

'Not possible,' answered Grandpa, casting a despondent gaze at his precious Concord, which now listed to the side, one front wheel buckled. He sounded defeated and humbled. I felt sorry for him.

'Any assistance I can give you before moving on?'

'Not really, Mr Campbell. But we'd appreciate some tonic. And thanks for your concern. To interrupt your run merely to help us is a most gallant act.'

'We'll secure the coach and follow you on our horses,' added Uncle Lenny.

'Don't let that Jefferson fellow get the better of you,' was Grandpa's parting advice to Mr Campbell.

A Surprise

I sat behind Uncle Lenny on Chomp Chomp with my legs dangling to one side, while holding onto Uncle Lenny's waist. Grandpa and Nunga rode on the two horses unhitched from the coach. We proceeded slowly, careful not to get into more difficulties. The track rose steadily towards the hills causing the horses to strain and sweat in the heat.

Wilkinson's Grocery Store & Bakery was located on a hillside next to a clump of mountain ash. Even from a little distance we could tell that a dozen or so people had gathered there. Some stood on the timber veranda of the store and others on the steps to the entrance. It was early afternoon, and the heat was at its peak. One of the drays made towards us, raising a trail of dust. A couple of yelping mongrel dogs followed, attempting to outrun the dray. It was Mr Atkinson and Mr Campbell come to commiserate.

'If it weren't for the accident, the Concord would certainly have outrun the drays and cart,' said Mr Campbell as he turned his dray around. 'But then,' he added as an afterthought, 'fortune is such a fickle thing. Wouldn't you say?'

Reaching the store, we were taken aback to see Mr Rodney. He limped to Grandpa as soon as we dismounted and apologised profusely. 'Didn't mean to cause you grief, Mr Cobb. You must believe me. How will I ever make amends?' He wrung his hands and wiped his brow, both arms and face covered in angry blisters.

'Come now, Mr Rodney, you weren't at fault. Not at all. What happened to us was an act of God. Let's leave it at that.' And I'd thought Grandpa intended to box his ears!

'Thanks, Mr Cobb, you're a considerate man like that there Mr Jefferson who found me lying on the exposed track in a parlous state and stopped and collected me.' Grandpa and Uncle Lenny raised their eyebrows and exchanged looks of surprise and disbelief.

Mr Atkinson mounted the stairs, took up a vantage point on the veranda and cleared his throat. All this while, Mr Jefferson was seated on a step, his knees pulled up to his chin and his head resting on his folded arms. One of the mongrels was now stretched out asleep on the lower step, ears twitching. 'Ladies and gentlemen, it falls upon my shoulders today to announce the winner of the race, a truly astounding result.'

'I wish he would be brief and have it done with,' mumbled Grandpa.

'Come up here, Mr Jefferson,' invited Mr Atkinson.

The man obliged with little visible enthusiasm. 'Ladies and gentlemen, Mr Jefferson's dray was first to arrive at Wilkinson's Grocery Store & Bakery.' With that he hoisted Mr Jefferson's reluctant right hand into the air. A few in the crowd clapped in an uncertain manner. Mr Jefferson burst into sobs, his shoulders heaving in spasms. I didn't feel sympathetically disposed.

'If I may take the liberty of explaining Mr Jefferson's emotional state,' continued Mr Atkinson. 'The poor man has been burdened by enormous pain and suffering since the loss of his wife to consumption. Now his infant child, bereft of a mother, is ill with croup.' Muffled sympathetic comments were heard. 'Mr Jefferson's been driven by desperation to find monies to pay for medical treatment for his child, for baby feed and to hire a wet nurse.' Mr Atkinson paused, wiped his brow and gazed past us as if he had stumbled upon a profound truth. Mr Jefferson at his side had stopped sobbing and raised his head for the first time presenting us a furrowed and forlorn face. A flood of guilt and shame washed over me like when Martha fell into the messy Yarro-Yarro.

'So you see now,' concluded Mr Atkinson, 'how the Almighty works His will in mysterious ways. Mr Jefferson here was clearly destined to win the twenty guineas pledged by Mr Swanson, the generous businessman.'

'Amen,' rose in unison from the crowd and, almost spontaneously, we all began singing 'Amazing Grace', our voices rising up from Notting Hill and lifting into the surrounding forest of eucalyptus and mountain ash. Noisy kookaburras fell silent, and a family of grazing kangaroos raised their heads and, momentarily, stood alert. Grandpa's voice, now clearly distinct, floated above all ours and echoed in the hills beyond.

I never felt so good.

The Patriotic Amnesiac

Robert New

The envelope was ordinary, a buff Manila pouch, sealed with fingerprint free sticky tape. The label had been written using a ruler to form the letters. It was addressed to Verity Trouver at WestNews. Verity looked at the envelope and frowned. This was only her second day at the newspaper.

Who knows I'm here? she wondered.

Opening the envelope revealed a single sheet of paper upon which a single word was written; *spray*.

Verity smiled wryly.

'At least you're interesting,' she said to the paper, as she stood up and began a brief, unsuccessful search for a spray bottle.

'There's always another way,' she whispered to herself, echoing her mother's often-used phrase.

Verity walked briskly to the lift, so preoccupied in her quest she barely noticed that she'd bumped into a colleague. Verity barely heard him mumble, 'You may have been head hunted to work here, but you don't have to be rude.'

Once Verity reached the balcony she switched on one of the fans that blew a mist of water to keep people cool in summer. She held the paper up to it and immediately words appeared on the page. Verity barely had time to read before the paper began disintegrating.

Within the secret branches of the government there is a person known as 'The Singularity.' The Singularity is a master of game theory and covert operations. People come to her safe in the knowledge that their discussions will never be repeated or told to anyone, even from other government agencies, regardless of the potential capture or interrogation of this person.

Their absolute certainty of the security of their conversations means they reveal all details regardless of their degree of classification. She alone has complete clearance. They receive unbiased and highly valuable strategic advice for covert operations.

The Singularity's impartiality and the security of what they reveal is based on two things:

1. *She only has a five minute memory due to the surgical removal of part of her brain.*
2. *She volunteered for the procedure.*

Her real name is classified, but I got to meet her last week and after meeting her and constructing an image of her face from memory, I found an image that identified her. I have reason to believe that she is your mother. Find her.

-A Friend

Verity's mind was reeling. *Mum! Five years of fruitless searching and then from nowhere a clue. Why now?* she thought.

Verity began pacing the balcony. The expansive

view of the city did not help her frustration.

Mum. You could be anywhere.

Verity frowned.

Surgical procedures mean records. Records mean clues. The surgeon would probably be an army doctor, so I've no chance of finding them ... I need to find Henry Silcove. He's the only anaesthetist Mum would've trusted. I haven't spoken to him in so long.

An internet search and two phone calls later and Verity was told that Henry would call her back when he was out of surgery. It was three hours later, when Verity was driving home, that her phone finally rang.

'Hello, this is Dr. Silcove, I'm returning your call.'

'*Salut*, Henry,' Verity said in an exaggerated French accent.

'Oh, so it's that Verity. Are you in the city?'

'Yes, King's P...'

'Meet me in an hour at the place where our families used to dine,' Henry interrupted.

'Okay,' Verity barely managed to reply before the call ended.

An hour later, Verity was sitting at a quiet table in *Parrhesia* restaurant sipping a coffee. She felt a rush of air as the door opened and looked up to see Henry walking towards her. Her eyes widened as he sat down.

'*Salut,* Verity. Yes, I know I'm a bit different: a lot greyer, balding and a bit thinner.'

'Henry, I can see ribs through your shirt. What the hell happened to you?' Verity momentarily forgot about her mother as concern for the person she used to affectionately call 'uncle' took over.

'Well, let's just say the last five years have not been kind, ever since I assisted your mother that day.' Henry paused and looked at Verity for confirmation.

‘Yes, I received a note that said Mum’d had some kind of surgery, and it implied that’s why she disappeared. You’re the only one she’d trust to anaesthetise her. Mum always said that anyone with the right procedural knowledge could repair someone, but that controlling someone’s pain, controlling their consciousness was an art. She thought you were a master.’

‘I was … I guess I still am, but I’m not the same person. I mean what they did to your mother that day… they took her from you, from everyone. They took her memory.’

‘That was what the note said. But what does that really mean? How do you take someone’s memory?’

‘The part of the brain that encodes information for storage in long-term memory is called the hippocampus, and there’s one in each half of the brain. They removed your mother’s hippocampi, well nearly all of each. As a result she only has the ability to hold new memories for a few minutes.’

Can she remember me? Verity found the thought too painful to ask.

‘So can she remember the past?’ she asked instead.

‘I think most of it; she knew she’d likely lose from months to years of memories from before the surgery. She worked for eleven years prior to the surgery to make sure she would remember what was needed afterwards, in case she lost more than anticipated.’

That explains how driven she always seemed and why she was both present and absent when I was growing up. But why hasn’t she contacted me? Wasn’t I what was needed?

‘When she woke up I asked her “what’s the last thing you remember?”’ Henry continued.

‘And?’

'She was a bit groggy, but she said something about the view from the hill. The sun rising over the mountains and the mist in the valleys.'

Our special place. Verity's hopes rose. Maybe her mother had needed her.

'Mum used to take me there every Sunday morning. *Oh, God*, she always used to say that she wanted to remember those moments forever.'

'Now you know why,' Henry said.

Verity frowned. 'I thought she was being cheesy… Do you know where she is?' she asked with a tinge of regret.

'No, I never saw or heard from her again.'

'So you can't tell me anything else?'

'No. Only that she thought it would be easier for you if she just disappeared.'

'Easier?' Verity felt an unexpected surge of anger. *How could Mum think this would be easier?* Henry saw the intake of breath and slight flaring of Verity's nostrils and reached for her hand.

'Yes. Think about how heartbreaking it would be being around her now — when she couldn't remember what day of the week it was, what year it was, or anything about the last five years. Everything that you would tell her would be lost and your relationship would be permanently stuck in the past. She would not be able to ask you how an important event went or show concern for dates or birthdays. People would notice the change in her and that would bring attention to her, which I'm guessing, given the non-disclosure forms I signed, would be a bad thing.'

Verity sighed. 'Yes, I guess so.'

'So, perhaps you can answer one thing for me?' asked Henry.

'Sure.'

‘Why did she do it? Why would she agree to have such a severe surgery,” Henry asked with such intensity that Verity realised he was getting himself into trouble by talking to her, but had to know the answer.

‘The note I received said that Mum works for the government. I have no idea what branch. But by removing her ability to form new memories, perhaps she became more useful to them.’

‘And your Mum was always so patriotic,’ Henry added.

‘Yes, country first, family second, religion third,’ Verity said by rote. Both her parents had drilled that into her since childhood.

‘Indeed,’ Henry sighed. ‘So what will you do now?’

‘Figure out a way to find her, I guess.’

‘Well, for what it’s worth I don’t think she told anyone else about the view. Maybe it was important to her for a reason?’

‘That’s possible. Given how much of a planner Mum was, if there is anything that is meant for me there, it would only reveal itself at what was our special time.’ Memories of their time at the lookout flooded over her and tears welled in her eyes.

‘Verity …’ Henry said, his throat catching the word.

‘Yes?’

‘She’d told me the surgery was for a tumour. She only told me the real reason during the surgery.’

‘During?’

‘Yes, she was conscious throughout,’ Henry replied.

No wonder Mum insisted on you, thought Verity.

‘It was the only way to know that they were operating in the right area. If I’d known what they were planning on doing … I’m so sorry. I would never…’

The remorse was evident in his voice.

'I know,' Verity said, reaching reassuringly for his hand. Henry moaned slightly. Verity stood up and gave him a slight hug.

'It's okay,' she whispered. 'It's not your fault.' Henry started sobbing as Verity gently kissed the top of his head.

'I have to go now,' Verity said, her voice suddenly hoarse. Henry nodded.

As soon as Verity was outside the restaurant, she broke down crying.

The next Sunday morning, Verity drove to the lookout at the top of a large hill near where they used to live. She arrived just before daybreak. The view was punctuated by streetlights in the twilight, until the sun's orange rays started shifting the palette of the scene. This was what she and her mother had found so enchanting; the kaleidoscopic shift in what they could see over the hour or so of the sun rising from behind the mountains, and the mist lifting in the valleys.

At the lookout was a rock with the inscription: *The truth shall set you free.*

The rock was on the other side of a balustrade and on the edge of a steep drop.

Verity remembered the rock being put there a year or so before her mother disappeared. Her mother had never really said anything about it, other than that it was a nice addition to the view.

But, since my name means truth, could this be a message for me? Verity wondered as she climbed over the balustrade and went closer.

As Verity looked at it now, she had the thought, *The 'the' seemed superfluous. Why include it unless it had another purpose?* The more she thought about it the more it seemed like the whole thing was meant for her.

Knowing Mum, it would be something obvious as she was fond of hiding things in plain sight. Verity gave a wry smile as she pressed each letter of the word truth in turn. Nothing happened. Verity frowned and then tried again. Still nothing. Finally she spelt 'truth' on the letters of set, free, you, the. This time the rock shifted back slightly from the edge of the cliff. Verity climbed onto the rock and looked over the edge, fighting back the vertigo that washed over her from the sight. The movement of the rock had revealed a slit in the ground beneath it that contained what looked like a memory card sealed in clear plastic that Verity could almost reach. She focused on the card and ignored the fall or what it would mean if she dropped it. She just managed to grasp the card and shuffle back from the edge. After Verity had stepped from the rock to climb over the balustrade, the rock slid back into its original place.

Verity decided to complete the old Sunday morning ritual she and her mother had shared. She drove to their favourite café and ordered Atlantic eggs and a cappuccino.

While she waited for her breakfast to arrive, Verity took out her laptop and inserted the memory card. There was a single file present, but when Verity tried to open it, it asked for a password.

Hmm, what would Mum set as a password if the file was meant for me?

She tried a few phrases and words without success.

Mum liked to hide things in plain sight, so what if the inscription on the rock, 'The truth shall set you free', was also a clue about the file? Oh, Mum, you were always one for telling me to be truthful. What was the phrase you used to use? Verily Verity? Verity smiled as she realised this could also be the file's way of asking if it was her.

Verity typed VerilyVerity as the password and the file opened. Verity smiled wryly. She always found her Mum's puzzles easier to solve than her father's.

My Darling Verity,

I am so sorry that I had to disappear from your life. I know it won't make any sense to you, but this is what was necessary for our country to improve the function of its intelligence organisations. By the time you get this I will be an amnesiac and unable to form new memories. As I would stand out and not be able to function properly in daily life, I've had to go into hiding. Rest assured, I will be well cared for, as will you be when I pass. I am assuming that if you read this, then your search for me has gone beyond 'grieving daughter' to something greater. If so, you can meet me at our special place on the Monday before your birthday each year (too much risk of seeing you accidentally on Sunday). You know what time. Please understand that I will not be the person you knew, nor will I know how much time has passed, so really think carefully about whether you want to meet me.

Love always,

Mum

Verity shook her head in disbelief. How could her mother possibly think that her daughter wouldn't want to see her?

Verity had to wait two months for the Monday before her birthday. Her mother was rarely out of her mind. She barely slept the night before, and made her way to the lookout a full hour before sunrise. It was still dark as she sat on the bench that overlooked the valley. As the first purple shimmer appeared on the horizon over the mountains, she became aware of a figure approaching. An older women who looked healthy and alert sat next to her.

'Mum!' Verity exclaimed.

'Hello, Verity. I had forgotten how beautiful you are. I have missed you. I love you.' Her mother took Verity's hand.

'Mum. I have so many questions.' Verity looked at her mother intensely.

'I may not be able to answer them. In a few moments I won't remember that we have spoken.'

'Really?'

'Yes. I can only learn new procedures — you know like muscle memory, even though I don't remember the event of learning the new information. I know this not because they told me so but because I expected that as an outcome of the surgery. But as you know, I always believe that there is another way. Seeing you is producing a strong emotional response in me so there is a chance…'

The bullet came from nowhere. It hit her mother's head in the back of her skull and travelled through her brain and out through her right eye socket. Blood spattered as far as the rock and its inscription. As her mother slumped forward, Verity screamed, 'MUM!'

When Verity returned to work two weeks later, she found another envelope on her desk. It was addressed the same way and contained another single sheet of paper. Verity took it straight to the misting fan and gasped as she read:

Singularities lie at the heart of black holes. Nothing is

meant to be able to escape a black hole's gravity. No information that goes in is meant to get out; thus it was the same with your mother no information she was told was meant to be able to get back out due to the surgery she'd had. Unfortunately, a few months ago, she found another way, just as physicists are trying to do for black holes now. She saw and kept a picture of you in the paper after your investigative success. There must have been just enough of her brain to enable the strength of the emotion produced to allow her to form a new memory. Thereafter, she was able to remember some things she was told by looking at your picture and adding the emotion generated to the memory. The extra intensity meant some of this information was then transferred to her long term memory. We realised she was doing this when she created a solution for an agency that showed knowledge she shouldn't have had. Her security was no longer assured. She was a true patriot, who put her country's needs above her own. She knew the risks going in and that if she were able to form new memories that she'd have to be eliminated. I'm sorry for our loss and involving you in tracking her.

Love,

Dad.

The Commander and the Beast

Olivia Oh

As an army commander, I stood on top of the hill for my early morning patrol. The sun kissed and lingered on my face, but the heat had never bothered me. If anything, I felt more energized.

A gentle breeze whisked past leaving the smell of fresh pine leaves in the air and red dirt swirling around me.

Loud thundering steps echoed from a distance, and the thumping rang in my ears. I saw the shadow come first, spreading across the land like wildfire.

Giant footsteps pounded closer. A beast with wild hair and a wicked grin was fast approaching.

I always knew this day would come.

My heart pounded as I sprinted back towards my kingdom. A few workers were building our castle, casually going about their day. They had no idea their lives were about to change. I could have warned them, but my first priority was to protect the queen. I raced towards her headquarters, noting two guards at the entrance.

‘Lord Commander,’ one greeted me with a small bow.

‘I need to speak to the queen.’

‘Her Majesty told us she is not to be disturbed.’

‘This is a call to arms. Unless you want to lose your head, step aside.’ I pushed past them. I didn’t have time for this.

Inside the chamber, the queen and her son were in deep conversation. There had been talks about forming an allegiance with another kingdom, and this was the subject under discussion. She always spoke with such quiet power that it made anyone pay attention.

‘Your Majesty.’ I bowed.

‘I gave strict instructions not to be interrupted.’ She scowled at me.

‘Salient alert!’

Her expression changed, and she motioned towards her son. ‘You may leave.’ He sighed, bowed, and left immediately. The queen turned to me. ‘You have my attention.’

‘A beast from the south is invading our lands, Your Majesty.’

‘What manner of a beast, Commander?’

I shook my head. ‘I’ve never seen a creature like it.’

‘Are you sure there is danger? We are located in the safest and most isolated place across the lands.’

‘Indeed. Yet we have been found.’

‘How far off is this beast?’

‘It is nigh.’

‘Then do what we’ve been training for. I’ll speak with the emissaries of the other kingdoms.’

I bowed and left the queen’s headquarters for the barracks where I sounded the alarms.

The troops were beside me within seconds.

'We are going to war.'

Agonising screams pierced the air. Everybody ran in different directions.

'Run to your homes,' I commanded the people, and they fled.

It was a fruitless effort. The beast had arrived. Its enormous feet kicked the kingdom, shattering it into ruins.

'Come out, come out wherever you are!' It grabbed one of the workers I saw earlier and crushed her.

The worker's mother wailed, shaking uncontrollably.

'Leave,' I exhorted.

Tears streamed down her face.

'Go!' I said again.

She hiccupped and sprinted away.

'Get into position,' I said to my army.

'Yes, sir!' they replied.

We marched in unison towards the evil creature. No one dared to breathe. We have been through horrific battles in our time, but none was ever like this.

'For the queen!' I yelled.

'For the queen!' they repeated.

We charged, but it didn't make a difference. The beast annihilated the front line soldiers without even flinching. They died in silence.

Soldiers around me lay injured, their bodies smashed into the ground.

This was no battle. It was a slaughter.

My queen arrived on the battlefield with thousands more soldiers. I smiled at the sight of our fearless leader doing what she does best: ruling and leading by example.

The morning light glowed around her.

'Attack!' she cried.

The soldiers roared and ran towards the gruesome beast.

It picked up one soldier and dangled him over its mouth. My comrade's end was a most horrible sound, which I'll never forget.

I felt my face flush with anger. *This is my home. These are my people.*

I ran, dodging the dead bodies around me. Body parts lay scattered everywhere. I stabbed the beast's foot, but it didn't even notice.

Its attention was on the queen.

I froze. It stood hovering around the queen. She stood high, standing her ground.

'Protect your queen,' I ordered.

I made my way to stand in front of her, attempting to provide a shield. There were not many of us now.

To my horror, I saw the beast pick her up and look at her curiously.

'I have the queen,' it snarled.

Without thinking, I grabbed onto the queen's legs. Wherever she goes I go, I reminded myself.

'Mummy, Mummy! Look what I've got!' The child waved a container excitedly.

'That's nice, darling. You caught a big one to add to your collection.' She ruffled his hair. 'Put it away. Breakfast is ready.'

As the child ran to his room, ants could be seen scurrying around in the container. One still held onto his queen.

A Receipt for Curing the Toothache

Andy Russell

Northgate, Halifax
Saturday September 9th 1848
This has been a very flat day in trade. Enough to make one feel almost at their wits end for want of a little more money and business. But what can one do. Only look to the Lord for resignation to his holy will trusting entirely in the providence of God for help and deliverance. Lord help me. I feel happy in the love of God and fully believe that he will keep me.

Jabus Smith carefully cleaned the pen nib on a piece of rag and closed his journal. Bare foot and wearing a nightshirt that hardly covered his ample stomach he doused the gas mantle and made his way from desk to bed navigating by touch. It was rare for Jabus's journal to include much of his daily comings and goings and this was especially true tonight. The most significant event of the day might not have preyed on his mind so much if he had committed it to his journal. As he lay in bed twisting and turning in a vain attempt to find a comfortable position he relived the events of that morning.

Salem Chapel was a brisk 5-minute walk from Anne Street, where Jabus lived over his grocery business. As usual on a Saturday he had gone to the chapel before opening up his shop. He needed to make sure that all was prepared for the Sunday services. The chapel stood in its own grounds and was built to a severe Calvinistic pattern: grey, rectangular and without colour or ornamentation. It embodied the rejection of religious symbols such as crosses, statues, stained-glass windows and flamboyant architecture. On approaching he was surprised to hear raised voices from behind the chapel. Curious, but somewhat fearful of what he might find, he edged forwards and peered cautiously around a corner of the building.

He was shocked to see the Minister, Isaac Simpson, and Patrick Bunting engaged in a most animated confrontation. Patrick was a rather short, heavy set, rotund person who seemed to be directing a stream of abuse at the Minister. His posture, arms held rigidly to his sides, was of someone barely controlling the impulse to lash out with his fists. He was red in the face and seemed about to suffer an apoplectic fit. By contrast the Minister was tall and spare with a deeply lined face and hollow cheeks. He had his open hands partly raised as though trying to calm the situation or perhaps fend off a blow. Jabus caught snatches of Patrick's contributions to the altercation:

'… you cannot do this to me ...'
'… nobody would believe you ...'
'… you will regret this …'

From a distance the Minister's replies were too

subdued to make out.

Jabus never could stand confrontation. In his nineteenth year his father passed away of typhus fever. As a result the young man fell even further under the dominating influence of his mother, a substantial woman with a fiery tongue. She saw off any young women who showed an interest in developing an association with the eligible young grocer. As directed by his mother, all of his energies were to be concentrated on the grocery business, his father's legacy. Later, when his mother too died of dropsy, Jabus came under the thrall of evangelical Methodism. After that, parading, singing hymns and preaching took all of his free time. Indeed these activities also occupied some of the time that he should have devoted to business.

Therefore, confronted by two eminent gentlemen on the point of coming to blows, Jabus withdrew quietly. Preparation of the chapel must wait until later in the day. He would have to close the shop for an hour on the busiest day of the week, but that could not be helped.

The Sunday 8 o'clock service was well attended. Jabus slipped into his customary pew towards the back of the congregation where he could supervise taking up of the collection. From there he had a diagonal view of Minister Simpson and his wife Isabel, seated in the front row. Jabus considered that the Minister's wife was quite the most striking woman in the congregation, demurely but not unattractively dressed, poised, and with the most charming features. He forced himself to look elsewhere and with a jolt realised that the whole of the left side of the Minister's face was swollen. Even from a distance he seemed to be bent over and in some pain. Jabus could not concentrate on the rest of the proceedings. Mr Reid, the second preacher, chose as his text *Examine yourself whether ye be in the faith.* After the final amen Jabus would have been unable to comment at all on this stirring oration.

Following the service Jabus moved to within earshot of the group of people gathered around the Minister. He was surprised and relieved to hear that the cause of the swelling was toothache and not as he had anticipated a blow to the head. Jabus had an idea and pushed himself forward.

“If the toothache is your problem then I have a most effective remedy,’ he offered. The Minister turned towards this new speaker. His face was wracked by pain and lack of sleep.

‘If you could let me have such a thing then I would be truly in your debt, Mr Smith.’

‘The chemist could make up the receipt on Monday. If I order the medication first thing in the morning, then my delivery boy could deliver the mixture to your home by mid-morning.’

There was a murmur of appreciation from the group. As Jabus turned to take his leave his eyes rested for a fraction of a second on a smile of gratitude from the Minister’s wife. That beautiful smile, a smile directed solely towards him, took his breath away. It became etched in his memory.

The following morning Jabus strode quickly down Crown Street. He hoped that his errand would not unduly delay opening his grocery business. The chemist shop window displayed a large mortar and pestle as well as two glass carboys of coloured liquid, one blue and the other red. Once inside Jabus was suddenly aware of a complex mixture of smells. Some of the aromas were familiar like soap, camphor and beeswax while others he could not place. The chemist, looked up from a ledger to address his first customer of the day.

'How can I be of assistance to you, Mr Smith?'

'Good morning to you Mr Priestly. You may know Mr Simpson our Minister at the Salem Chapel? He is greatly troubled by the toothache and I have undertaken to provide a suitable medication.'

At mention of the Minister's name the chemist's genial expression hardened. After some thought he replied, 'I will do this for you but not because of any kindly thoughts towards the Minister.'

Jabus was taken aback by this reply and with some hesitation handed over a piece of paper. It read:

A receipt for curing the toothache
2 drams of alum well powdered
7 drams of nitrous spirit of ether
mix them together then apply them to the gums

A price of one shilling and half an hour to make up the receipt were agreed. Jabus paid in advance. Zeke, his delivery boy, would return in half an hour to pick up the medication.

After opening up his grocery store Jabus prepared for the all too infrequent customers. When all was in order Jabus sent Zeke to collect the medication and deliver it to the Minister's house. As a youngster Zeke had suffered an almost uninterrupted succession of ailments. Stunted growth, a weak heart and very limited education left him with few avenues for employment. However, these limitations were somewhat compensated by a cheeky smile. As a kindness to a fellow member of the Salem Chapel Jabus had agreed to employ Zeke for a three-month trial. He was employed as delivery boy and general helper around the store. Zeke was a willing worker but was hardly capable of following even the simplest of instructions. This was particularly the case if they involved anything he had not encountered before. Therefore, it was not particularly surprising to Jabus when Zeke arrived back at the grocery store in an agitated state. He had the medication but could not find where to deliver it. In exasperation Jabus sent Zeke on another delivery to an address with which he was familiar.

That will keep him occupied, Jabus thought as he donned his coat. He placed a sign stating *Closed for 20 minutes* in the window, locked up and set out to deliver the medicine himself. Striding through the streets he could not help congratulating himself. The assistance he was providing for the Minister could do nothing but improve his standing at the chapel.

The Minister's house was a short way out of town, further than he had anticipated. Perhaps it was not so surprising that Zeke had failed to find it. The house itself was small and neat with a well-kept garden. Jabus recognised hydrangeas and patches of delphiniums, peonies and geraniums edging a stone path to the front door. His first knock seemed to go unanswered. He was still of two minds whether to knock again or return later when the door was opened by Isobel Simpson. She smiled to see him, that same smile. Again Jabus felt that he could not catch his breath and must surly die of asphyxiation. Fortunately, Isobel started talking without any prompting. This gave Jabus a few moments to regain his composure. It transpired that although in extreme discomfort the Minister had felt bound to attend the sickbed of one of the older members of the chapel. Would Jabus like to step inside and wait? At that moment the offer was what he most wanted and what he most feared. His mind was in an absolute panic. All he could think to do was thrust the small blue medicine bottle into her hands and make a hasty and incoherent retreat. The chemist had attached a label to the bottle with the receipt and instructions so no explanation was really necessary.

About lunchtime the terrible news spread through the town of Halifax. Isaac Simpson, Minister of the Salem Chapel, had suffered a violent seizure in front of his wife and was dead before anyone could render assistance. He had been unwell with a bad toothache. However, there was nothing that could have forewarned of a fatal seizure.

In the afternoon Jabus received word of a meeting at the chapel and had no interest in keeping the business open. Zeke was disappointed when he was told to go home because his mother needed every day's pay, little as it was. His mood brightened when Jabus assured him that he would be paid for the full day anyway. A large sign was hung in the window explaining that as a mark of respect for the recently deceased Minister of Salem Chapel the business would be closed for the rest of the day. Jabus then made straight for the hastily convened prayer meeting. The gathering was very well attended but notably absent was the Minister's wife, Isabel. The word was that she would remain isolated at home for some days in case the cause of the Minister's affliction proved infectious. After the assembly sang a few appropriate hymns Jabus was gratified to be invited to give an oration. He chose as his text *Blessed are they that mourn, for they shall be comforted.*

As the meeting dispersed Patrick Bunting indicated that he would like a private word concerning the business of the United Order of the Peaceful Dove. Mention of the work of the friendly society produced a sudden anxious reaction. Jabus felt a sinking feeling in his stomach. Although the chapel was far from well heated a sweat broke out on his forehead.

'As you will recall, during our meeting at the Golden Plough Inn last week we had fresh receipts of £14-5-11½?' Patrick's eyebrows arched upwards to emphasise the question. 'I seem to remember that sick members were paid out £1-10-6½. Also, final funeral expenses of £2-6-3 were allocated to Mr Thomas's widow to cover his coffin, grave and hearse?'

Jabus already knew where this conversation was heading.

'Looking into the accounts it seems that there is a £5 shortfall in the funds to hand.' There was a long silence and when Jabus failed to respond Patrick continued. 'I am sure that there is some perfectly reasonable explanation for the discrepancy.' This latter statement was spoken without conviction. 'I expect you to put things to rights straight away!'

With this Patrick turned on his heel and left Jabus alone with his thoughts. It was true that the quarterly rent for the shop had fallen due. Because of a number of weeks of poor sales he did not have the £8 and 5 shillings rent to hand by the due date. However, the store had stock and he fully expected trade to pick up so that he could return the money to the friendly society. That night he confided his problems to his journal. As usual, there was no specific mention of the root causes.

Monday September 11th 1848

This has been a day of much trial of mind and temptation from Satan. How much need I have to be on my watch against the assaults of the enemy and the corruption of my heart. I mourned all this day, and I was brought into great heaviness through the deceitfulness of sins. Lord God have mercy upon me.

The following day started with the promise of some fine weather. The clouds had cleared and the sun was drying out the puddles of overnight rain. In the morning Jabus received a chest of black tea from Sunderland & Co., Tea Dealer of London. Because there were no deliveries to be made, Jabus set Zeke to work measuring out quarter-pound lots of tea into paper packets. Each packet was started with a spoon full of tea dust retained from the bottom of a previous chest. Nobody would buy the dust on its own but it was hardly noticed at the bottom of a full packet of tea. Each packet was then filled to weigh exactly a quarter pound, but no more.

At first Jabus didn't recognise the hunched woman who entered the shop. She was wearing a shabby coat and headscarf and carried a large basket. Once inside the store, and sure that there were no other customers, she stood up straight and motioned to a quiet corner out of earshot of Zeke. Jabus let out an involuntary gasp of surprise when he recognised Isobel Simpson.

'I came to warn you,' she began, looking out into the street to ensure that they were not observed. 'The constable came to the house this morning. He asked a lot of questions, questions about the Minister's toothache and the seizure that killed him.' Her eyes filled with tears as she thought back to those events.

Jabus offered his handkerchief and then instantly regretted that it was some days since it had been laundered.

'The constable also asked about the United Order of the Peaceful Dove,' she said frowning. 'I cannot imagine why. As you know it was my husband who dealt with that. I had no involvement.'

Staring into her vulnerable, tear streaked face Jabus could think of nothing to say. Instead he placed a supporting hand on her shoulder. 'The constable also took away several of my husband's things including the bottle of toothache medicine. He said that there were suspicions that the Minister might have been poisoned.' With this last statement Isobel dissolved into a flood of tears and against his better judgement Jabus found himself holding her in a comforting embrace.

In the evening, after closing the shop, Jabus did something that he had not done for a long time, in fact not since his mother died. He took the gently sloping path through fields and up the slope to Beacon Hill overlooking Halifax. He was rewarded with a wonderful view over the houses, factories and woollen mills of the town. Up there he could smell that the air was so much cleaner, the sun a little brighter. As he leaned on a farm gate and surveyed the town he considered his situation. It didn't seem to be a very good situation. If it transpired that the Minister had been poisoned by the toothache medicine then things looked very bleak indeed.

He reasoned that, although not true, some people might think that he had stolen money from the United Order of the Peaceful Dove. In fact he considered it as only a short-term loan that he fully intended to repay. Could such a short-term loan be misconstrued as a motive to commit murder, he thought? He had heard of people being murdered for the small change in their pocket. Would people believe that £5 would be sufficient to induce a stalwart of the community such as himself to commit murder? If this was the case then it would be a motive for murder. If it transpired that the bottle of medicine contained poison then this must have been the means by which the murder was carried out. The bottle was directly linked to him for he had ordered and paid for it. Finally, he carried the bottle to the minister's home. This gave him the opportunity to add the poison and hence commit the crime.

Looking at all of the facts of the situation it was difficult to see how any fair minded person could doubt that he had killed the Minister. Having reached this conclusion Jabus looked out over Halifax and the surrounding country with a fresh measure of appreciation. Would this be the last time he would be free to admire the view from the hill?

The View from the Hill

A short story from the *The Sonic Flu* (forthcoming) by Robert Sayegh

Numa woke just before the first sunrays hit the top of the cliff behind her forest cabin. The lights of dawn in pale grey and blue were spreading among the scattered clouds. She felt dreamily refreshed after a long, lazy sleep and couldn't remember the last time she'd slept so well. A melody was playing in her head.

The melody her brain was relentlessly humming was Tchaikovsky's *The Nutcracker*, and this puzzled her as she struggled into her waking state, as she rarely felt puzzlement at all. She sat violently upright, fully awake now, pushing her puzzlement into a secluded corner of her mind, while sharpening all her senses to deal with whatever had come upon her this morning.

A worry crept into her mind. Was she infected with the sonic flu?

She tried to make a rational and objective assessment: was she dreamily humming the music, energized by the mountain's refreshing air? Or was her brain merely resonating, compelled to keep track with a humming inflicted upon it by the virus?

She sprang to the shower, stepping under freezing water, which was pumped fresh into her cabin from the nearby melting snow capes. The low temperature should slow the virus' activity. This would not stop the virus' energy, as de-noising and eliminating its impact was practically impossible as far as everyone knew. But slowing it might give her enough time to ponder the situation at hand.

This cabin was the only asset she'd kept of her parents' inheritance. In her childhood it had been their family's summer vacation home. Her mother had been a highly successful marketing executive for the biggest IT company in what used to be called the country of England. At work and at home she'd been a dedicated, punctual, effective and seriously calculated woman, but not in this cabin. In this cabin, Numa observed in awe and joy how summer after summer her mother would suddenly become a relaxed, warm and joyful person. It was as if a part of her would hibernate and would only unfold within the confinement of this cabin.

Numa didn't keep the cabin for the sake of these beautiful memories. Sentiment had nothing to do with it. Hints of the world crisis that had emerged twelve years ago, the collapse of political states as they had been known for almost two centuries before, and latest news about an impeding epidemic catastrophe had made her realise her best insurance policy for independence and survival was to keep such a secluded and far away hideout — and so she had.

So how could she have caught the sonic flu virus when she was alone here? One part of Numa's mind retreated to deal with this shocking question, while her senses still resurrected the pleasant past, flavoured by smells from the blooming spring of the raising dawn outside the cabin, mixed with her memories of dewy summer fields. *The Nutcracker* was still circulating in her head, her mind humming with flutes and violins.

Memories of her mother emerged, and she remembered watching her sit for hours painting the views while listening to classic music — most affectionately to Tchaikovsky's works.

Numa realised her mind wasn't experiencing a wave of random affectionate memories about her childhood. She was trying to bootstrap a solution, to dig out, unfold and decipher the unwrought message that her subconscious had somehow already solved!

The chill water kept pouring on her head and shoulders, and although her skin was accustomed to cold showers she felt annoyed that the water was almost freezing, and she grew agitated. Hence, she concluded it wasn't the temperature of the shower that annoyed her, but the factor of this unexpected situation that sent her emotions spiralling out of control.

In her imagination, she scanned the view around the cabin seeking the recognition of something, the view from the hill, the cliffs around, the deep dark forest, and the creek below; but nothing special caught her attention. Focusing on the cabin again, her conscious mind cried in excitement, Music! Of course.

Instinctively, she stormed out of the shower, not even concerning herself to shut off the water, leaving a wet trail on the cabin's floor. She headed back to the main hall, and pushed herself up onto her tiptoes to reach the upper shelf of the closet there. Here she found the CD player along with her mother's audio collections, nestled in a decorative wooden box.

Soon she'd find out for sure what was going on. She

had to act fast. A CD player! That was quite a tricky course of action to think about in the first place. Luckily no one had visited this place for years, and she'd forgotten all about the music collection, otherwise it would have been destroyed like the rest of the collections around the world, or was it not forgetfulness?

Who could have imagined a mere five years ago that recording music was about to be banned by the newly formed WN (Worldwide Nations) and that the ban would be enforced under the most severe international laws as a war crime, no less. Although music itself hadn't been banned, any form of electronic systems that recorded, stored, or played it had been. Nowadays, music bands were still permitted to play, as long as they used acoustic devices without any electronic aid.

The sonic flu wasn't an epidemic, not yet, especially as researchers found that it infected individuals without a pattern, and for some reason it didn't seem to be contagious. Although some recorded cases had shown person-to-person transmission, as if the sonic flu had bounced back from one recipient to another.

In any case, until researchers figured out the origin and a possible cure or vaccination, authorities had banned recorded music to make sure the worst-case scenario was a sonic flu that could only infect one person at a time, even if anyone found a way to make the virus airborne through electronic aids, where it could possibly infect the masses.

Numa would have to decide what to do with this illegal CD and the music collection later, but first things first. She soon found *The Nutcracker* CD, "Deluxe Edition". The pale cover still held the dignified old shades of an elegant brownish colour.

While preparing the music, her mind recalled the essential known facts about the virus. The Sonic Flu, as people started to call it, wasn't really a flu, and it probably wasn't a virus either. But no one knew how it had come about, when it started, or whether its origin was the unthinkable — a man-made engineered viral weapon.

Its victims were witnessed as dying suddenly and peacefully, after suffering from the flu. But accumulated cases of autopsy started revealing a more accurate yet darker turn of events. It was found that those infected had suffered intense vibrations inside their heads, such vibrations that resonated and interfered with the brain waves.

After the sonic flu infected someone, they would keep hearing this sonata inside their heads, which would begin like a harmless earworm, but one that wouldn't disappear for days. Gradually the person would develop symptoms of flu: fever, nausea and a headache; however, no medicine could possibly treat it. Those infected, would literally be humming their lives away as the sonic flu fed on their brain waves, while inflicting an unstoppable ear work, forcing a humming into the brain, loop feeding on its energy, and gradually forcing the brain activity to a terminal shutdown, until the victim finally fell into an irreversible coma, where only primal motoric sensory kept working, but no conscious activity of the brain could be revived. Within the first three hours of infection, the subject would start humming a song, the last one they would hear.

Hurriedly, Numa played the track *Dance of the Sugar Plum Fairy*. Standing still in the middle of the room, she closed her eyes while the violin's sharp yet gentle strokes intensified in tune with the echoes inside her skull, followed by the definitive sounds of the enigmatic bells that soon took over and penetrated her senses. She hugged her chest and felt her breathing increasing with the rise of the violin sounds, felt raising alarm at the idea of upcoming danger. She summoned all of her attention and listened to the track thoroughly, then played it again.

Now that she'd synced the music from the CD player along with the humming inside her brain, it was time to examine her fears; this time she chose to play her favourite track, *Dance of the Reed Flutes*. Many years had passed since she'd last heard it, and she hoped it wouldn't be the last. She listened carefully, endorsing the chirpy flutes with a message of hope, the dance of violins, feeling pure bliss, then a suspension and anticipation, a fear that her hope was premature and never meant to be her destiny; she could never completely control her emotions while listening to this track. The music flowed and engulfed her subconscious and she emerged back into her thoughts: Voilà! 'I just woke up with earworms this morning,' she convinced herself, as the new tune took over and her brain changed its humming to the new melody. She was not infected. She exhaled a relieved breath.

Happy with this turn in events, while the sounds of flutes, violins and bells still filled the cabin, she started to feel the chill breeze of the morning impinging her naked, wet body, and headed back to the shower turning on the hot water this time.

She let herself relax for a few seconds and unwind the built tension. She kept humming the music, while enjoying her luck at probably being the only person on earth who could listen to music in private after so many years. The shower steam warmed her body and soul, and she smiled trying to remember if she still had the

‘In Time’ album from the band she liked, “View from the Hill”.

A Life of Wonderful Views

Gordon J R Smith

In no other capital city of Australia does the Great Dividing Range, its satellite ranges and minor summits, form such a marvellous skyline as that when viewed from many high points around Melbourne, Doncaster, Wheelers Hill and above the Austin Hospital in Heidelberg. This extensive panorama is never the same from day to day, varying in shades of blue and grey with the changing cloud cover and weather conditions. This 180-degree skyline panorama extends from Mt Disappointment in the northwest above Whittlesea, ending at One Tree Hill in the southeast above Ferntree Gully. There are a variety of mountain peaks to be seen, some over 900m high, the highest being Lake Mountain at just over 1400m. When viewed from Heidelberg above the Austin Hospital, if one turns around, the continuation of Great Dividing Range with Mt Macedon to the west can be observed.

I can remember one very hot night in the summer of 1939 when our family walked to the top of our street, Hillside Road, to see if we could see any evidence of the fires that were reported to be burning in the mountains. Looking to the east, through the blackness, we saw lovely, twinkling, orange lights in the east. They were in fact the colours of the devastating January 13th bushfires of 'Black Friday', burning in the Dandenong Ranges. These terrible bushfires raged across Victoria, destroying much of our pristine eucalypt forests, together with many towns and villages. Industries were destroyed, particularly the logging mills, their infrastructure and their settlements, which housed those who lived and worked on the milling operations and in which some of them lost their lives. A total of 71 people died in the Black Friday fires, and 3,700 buildings were destroyed.

Sometime after the bush fires had come to an end, looking across at the ranges, I was surprised to see what I first thought had been a fall of snow, but it was the sun shining on burnt trees, many of which had white trunks.

In the wintertime it is always a great thrill for me if viewing conditions are favourable. If I strain my eyes or with the aid of binoculars I am able to see the snow on Lake Mountain where I skied in 1951. Every time that I gaze at the many mountain peaks on this magnificent skyline, it brings back many happy memories of the times I visited and climbed many of these summits. Such is my love affair with the mountains: in my 90th year, ardent admiration from a distance, but no less fervent than in my earlier years.

Many years ago, backpacking in the winter of 1952, I spent two weeks in Vienna and visited the famous Vienna Woods, located very nearly the same distance from Vienna as the Dandenong Ranges are from Melbourne. Like the Dandenong Ranges they also have two summits, which are virtually the same heights as those on the Dandenongs. The view from the Vienna Woods with Vienna in the distance and the Danube close by, which on that day really was blue, reflecting the sky above, made quite a panorama of contrast with snow covered vineyards in the foreground.

The views from the Dandenong Ranges on the other hand, with the Great Dividing Range to the north and west, and Port Phillip Bay to the south are a very much broader view than that from the Vienna Woods. In my opinion the Dandenong Ranges are by far, much more attractive, with regards the variety of forestry, local points of interest, views and overall beauty. I believe that this is still so, as I write. The Dandenong Ranges only lack the history and the musical connections that the Vienna Woods are famous for.

Continuing on with my backpacking tour, I crossed and recrossed the European Alps in Italy, Switzerland and France at various locations. The European Alps, like the Great Dividing Range, divide and direct the rain that falls on them into famous rivers. However, both mountain ranges differ markedly in scale in two important respects: the Great Dividing Range is 3500 km long and its highest point is Mt Kosciusko 2228m, while the European Alps, which rise first in the Vienna Woods, are only 1100 km long and after winding their way through the southern countries of Europe, come to an end diving into the Mediterranean Sea around Nice and Cannes on the Cot d' Azure.

The European Alps contain many mountains with summits over 4000m high, most with permanent snow cover, the highest being Mt Blanc in France at 4809m. I skied for three weeks in Switzerland and from the balcony of the restaurant at the top station of the rack railway from Zermatt, there is a stupendous 180-degree view of the European Alps. The view from this balcony was once described as the *'Royal Box of the Mountain Theatre'* and it certainly is.

The magnificent skyline of the Alps that one sees from this balcony of the Gornergrat restaurant is close to a 180-degree arc. This awesome skyline marks the border between Italy and Switzerland, in which there are seven mountain peaks whose summits are over 4000m high. These are called the '*Four Thousanders.*' One of these, Monte Rosa, the highest mountain in Switzerland at 4634m, shares its summit with Italy. The most spectacular, however, is without doubt the mighty Matterhorn, its final, awesome, north face, rising abruptly before dropping steeply down to the last of the four thousander summits. I took many photos of this magnificent panorama, pinching myself to make sure it was truly me there in real life and not a dream!

Later in the week, I ski toured with a German companion up the Theodule Glacier to the Theodul Pass, at 3295m from where I looked down the very steep, icy slopes of the pass into the Aosta Valley in Italy. It was the most exciting ski tour I have ever made, skiing around the last 1200m of the Matterhorn's towering height of 4478m.

I have climbed and visited many of the summits of both mountain chains by various means and marveled at God's landscapes below my feet, but those, which I have climbed by my own laborious steps, have left me with more lasting and rewarding memories.

An approximate 20° section of the view from Doncaster Shopping Town car park, with the names of the mountains and their heights

The view down into the Aosta Valley in

Italy from the Theodule Pass in Switzerland

The View from the Vienna Woods The Danube River can just be seen at the left hand edge of the photo

The author and the view of the European Alps from the balcony at the Gornergrat

About the Authors

Bishnu Addison

Bishnu is a retired high school teacher. Her hobbies are writing, reading crime fiction and the classics. She's a self-confessed writing workshop 'junky' hunting for gems. She joined the Monash Writers Group when it was first established in 2013. The monthly meetings facilitated initially by David McLean and then by Margaret Hepworth have fuelled motivation and interest in writing. Her highlight of the meetings are when fellow writers share their work with the group and inspire the rest of them. She wishes to thank Sandhya Burton, Pamela McGowan, the Monash Council, and Wheelers Hill library staff for the venue and support.

Email: b.addison@bigpond.com

Nikki Bielinski

I like travelling to different countries and corners of the world. I also like travelling to different realms and regions in story worlds, in my mind and on the page.

As I'm often inspired by random ideas or incidents, the fiction I write is across the spectrum of age groups and genres. These stories are being largely stockpiled until I'm discovered!

I've had several adult short stories published. Though I usually write quirky picture books for children, or fantasy young adult fiction, sometimes, just sometimes, there is a vengeful ghost who wants their story to be heard.

http://spilttheink.blogspot.com.au/

Sasha Buntman

Passionate about communicating and organising, I've always felt compelled to write. As a Virtual Authors' Assistant, I'm involved in the writing, editing, publishing, design and marketing of clients' publications. My purpose has always revolved around the art of organising: organising the layout of elements on a page or in a book, or organising words, sentences and messages to create something meaningful. In various ways, I have created positive changes, helped people to learn and grow, and transformed perspectives. I have a media degree, diplomas in business, writing, editing and desktop publishing, and also worked at Fairfax Media for 5+ years.
www.midnightmedia.com.au

Katharina Fares

Katharina Fares was born in a German-speaking settlement of Hungary. She grew up in Communist East Germany and moved to West Germany where she studied fashion design and clothing manufacturing.

After coming to Australia she worked as a Designer in the fashion industry and established her own manufacturing and retail business. Later, she obtained a Dip. Ed. and a B. Ed. She lectured and wrote curriculum documents in her field of expertise.

She has written many short stories and poems and during 2016 published a novel: **View from a Barred Window** (ISBN 798-0-9945680-0-7)

Katharina is currently writing her second historical novel. She is married with three adult children and lives with her husband in Melbourne.

Sakuntala Gananathan

Sakuntala is a retired chartered accountant. The above story is an extract from her historical novel, "White Flowers of Yesterday," which was awarded Editor's Choice by her publishers, iUniverse. An excerpt of their appraisal: "The author has done a fantastic job of weaving setting, characterisation, historical information, dialogue, and plot together to create a complete, unique and compelling story…"

"…a surfeit of grace and wit." Kirkus Review.

Mend a Bend earned her a prize at the Monash Word Fest Short Story Competition in 2013.

https://www.facebook.sakuntala.gananathan
http://saku.teamfours.com

S.C Karakaltsas

S.C Karakaltsas lives in Melbourne and began writing in 2014 after many years in corporate life. She wrote and published her first novel called *Climbing the Coconut Tree* in March 2016. Inspired by true events on an island in the Central Pacific in 1949, the novel is a tale of a naive young man who stumbles into a world of violence and murder.

Her collection of short stories called *Out of Nowhere* is due out in 2017. Her short story, *The Surprise* was shortlisted in the Lane Cove Literary Awards 2016.
https://sckarakaltsas.wordpress.com/
Twitter @SKarakaltsas

Bala Mudaly

Bala Mudaly is a psychologist and still working at the age of 78 years. Oakleigh has been his home for the past 27 years, since he migrated from South Africa with his wife. Bala is partial to writing essays and short stories, which are usually set in Oakleigh and surrounding South Eastern suburbs. He took up writing as a hobby two years ago when he noticed a slow decline in his spelling and creative writing skills. He is particularly fascinated with how characters in fiction come into being, take on a persona of their own, and often outlive their creator.

Email: nmudaly@optusnet.com.au
M: 0414761663

Robert New

Robert is the author of *The Conversationist* and *Incite Insight* (ISBN: 978-0994439901) and is currently working on a collection of short stories to be published mid-2017. According to his wife, Robert has spent too much of his life studying. She has a point as he holds seven tertiary qualifications. Robert has degrees in psychology, sociology, biology and education, all of which inspire his writing. He likes writing stories that involve science and that shift the perspective of the reader. Due to a joke escalating a little too quickly, he once became a state finalist in an interpretive dance competition, but chickened out and did not go.

robertsnew.com
Twitter @1RobertNew

Olivia Oh

Olivia Oh has been a freelance copywriter for various media companies over the years. She has recently become a finalist for this story 'The Commander and the Beast' for the Monash Short Story Writing Competition.

Olivia's passion for writing started when she completed school work experience at the *Herald Weekly Times*. Furthermore, she enjoyed studying the short writing courses at RMIT University: Writing Creative Fiction (parts 1 & 2) and Writing for Children, as well as numerous other writing workshops.

She is a keen subscriber and member of Buzzwords, Writers Victoria and Romance Writers of Australia.

Andy Russell

Two years ago Andy Russell retired as an electronics engineer. At school English was one of his least favourite subjects. Now, after years of technical writing, it does not seem so bad after all. As one of his retirement activities he is enjoying writing fiction.

Gordon J R Smith

Gordon J R Smith was born in 1927 in Victoria. He qualified as a tradesman fitter and turner in 1949 with the Victorian Railways. He was a Rover Scout and member of the Youth Hostels Association. In 1952 he sailed abroad to the UK on a working and backpacking holiday, returning to Australia in 1953. He worked, married and raised a family on the Kiewa Hydro-Electric Scheme for 10 years. Returning to Melbourne, he worked for 18 years with General Electric. When GE close he taught Fluid Power at the Royal Melbourne Institute of Technology, from where he retired in 1993. He has written and published books about his travels abroad and working life.

www.ingramcontent.com/pod-product-compliance
Lightning Source LLC
Chambersburg PA
CBHW021023120726
47905CB00009B/3146

* 9 7 8 0 9 9 4 4 3 9 9 5 6 *